TUFF LU

Nick was
Warehous
looked beautiful and lost with dark tracks
of tears and mascara on her cheeks.
Morgan, she implored silently, *don't
come. I don't care anymore, but Nick's
gonna kill you. Stay away. . .*

But just then Morgan came swinging out
of the balcony on a rope. The second
he hit the stage, he and Nick were on the
floor, grappling like wild animals. . .

Then there was a click. Frankie was
standing over them both, holding a pistol
cocked to fire. She was crying, but her
hands weren't trembling. She had made
her choice, Morgan could see it in her
eyes. . . .

Bestselling SIGNET VISTA Books

TUFF TURF

by
Karen S. Marc

A SIGNET BOOK

NEW AMERICAN LIBRARY

PUBLISHER'S NOTE

This novel is a work of fiction. Names, characters, places, and incidents either are the product of the author's imagination or are used fictitiously, and any resemblance to actual persons, living or dead, events, or locales is entirely coincidental.

NAL BOOKS ARE AVAILABLE AT QUANTITY DISCOUNTS
WHEN USED TO PROMOTE PRODUCTS OR SERVICES.
FOR INFORMATION PLEASE WRITE TO PREMIUM MARKETING DIVISION,
NEW AMERICAN LIBRARY, 1633 BROADWAY,
NEW YORK, NEW YORK 10019.

Acknowledgment
"We Walk The Light" © 1984. Written by Jonathan Elias.
Published by Chilly D. Music and Music Design Publishing.
Used by permission.

SIGNET TRADEMARK REG. U.S. PAT. OFF. AND FOREIGN COUNTRIES
REGISTERED TRADEMARK—MARCA REGISTRADA
HECHO EN CHICAGO, U.S.A.

SIGNET, SIGNET CLASSIC, MENTOR, PLUME, MERIDIAN AND NAL BOOKS
are published by New American Library,
1633 Broadway, New York, New York 10019

First Printing, January, 1985

1 2 3 4 5 6 7 8 9

PRINTED IN THE UNITED STATES OF AMERICA

PROLOGUE

Frankie Croyden was anything but old-fashioned, even though she had a face that could have been lifted from a sepia-tinted photograph and blond hair that fell down her back, almost meeting the hem of her short clingy red dress. Frankie walked up to the bus stop, startling the man with the briefcase, and counted the seconds before she launched into her routine . . . 8, 9, 10.

Now.

Pretending to be oblivious to the man's fascinated glances, Frankie plowed through her purse, looking for bus fare. She pulled out a five-dollar bill and looked at the man in disbelief. For extra effect, she flashed him an innocent smile.

"Excuse me, sir . . . I was wondering if you had change for a five?"

"Sure!" The man pulled a wad of bills from his pocket.

"Oh, great," Frankie said. Great, Frankie thought. Another sucker done for. Please don't let it take too long.

Frankie glanced down the alley, looking for her best friend, Ronnie, who stepped out of the shadows and grinned. Ronnie pulled a beer bottle out of her purse and waved it in the air.

That was the signal Nick Hauser had been waiting for.

Nick was hanging out. He looked like any kid on a dark wet street at night, waiting for his friends to finish leafing through the piles of girlie magazines. But after one look at his face, anyone could see he was the kind of guy you'd hate to meet if your car died on a deserted street late at night. Nick's friends were his gang members. They weren't really reading magazines; they were waiting for the signal too, waiting like a pride of lions ready to go in for the kill.

"Yo." Nick snapped his fingers and the Tuffs dropped their magazines, primed for action. Nick took inventory and grinned. First of all, there was Eddie. Eddie was alert and observant, the silent type, quick and effective.

And fast-fingered Mickey, busy as usual with his can of spray paint. The kid was hyper as hell, but he had eyes like a hawk and the graffiti logos he left in his wake kept his nerves from getting jangly. Mickey loved the feel of the paint whooshing out of his can. It felt almost as good as holding a straight razor.

Nick snapped his fingers again and the gang moved quickly across the street. One of the Tuffs broke off a car antenna on the way, slashing it through the air to test its weight. The gang moved like a machine through the night, stilettos clicking open, power flowing, the antenna snapping in time to their footsteps.

The man at the bus stop moved closer to Frankie. "I still think it's too late for you to be out alone."

"Oh." She smiled coyly. "I'm not alone. You're here." She pretended not to see the approaching gang. This was getting too dangerous; she'd done it too many times.

"Yeah, but *I* wouldn't be here if my car wasn't in the garage getting a tune-up . . ."

Nick was on the man in a flash, grabbing him by the throat and pushing him back into a fence. Frankie moved out of the way. She'd done her job—now all she had to do was watch the gang in action. Nick was casually angling his stiletto into the man's cheek.

"Look in the left-hand jacket pocket," the man said in a strangled whisper.

"Get it," Nick ordered Frankie.

Frankie walked over to the man and looked straight into his eyes as she reached for his wallet, but as she touched his sports jacket, her hand faltered.

"Shit!" Nick tightened his grip on the man and scowled at Frankie just before he glanced down the street to see what had stopped her.

It was just this guy on a bike, singing bebop at the top of his lungs. Some dumb preppie in the wrong place at the wrong time.

They all watched as the guy on the bike took the setup in a flash, everyone frozen, surprised into shock. The preppie had to make a decision.

Morgan went into action, riding his bike into the middle of the gang. He kicked out with his right foot, knocked the nearest Tuff over, and wheeled away from an open knife. Then Morgan grabbed the beer bottle out of Ronnie's hand, shook it fiercely, and yelling "Rain from heaven," sprayed it into Mickey's eyes. Mickey screamed, stumbling back, and on his fall he accidentally jammed the nozzle of his spray-paint can. A thick stream of black acrylic slashed across Nick's face.

The man grabbed his briefcase and ran as Nick screamed in anger and frustration. Eddie was paralyzed. Frankie couldn't believe what was happening.

Her eyes connected with Morgan's and she took two involuntary steps backward. The guy on the bike regained his balance just in time to face the last standing Tuff, who was wielding the car antenna like a B-movie ninja. Morgan saw him coming and swerved in time. He got away. Almost.

The antenna slashed through the Japanese patch on the back of Morgan's leather bomber jacket, splitting it in half, jaggedly dividing the letters from the image of a rising sun.

> To influence the lives of men
> One must remain outside the circle of
> forces which affect them

If the Tuffs had known what the symbols meant, they could have cared less. Nick was in a fury beyond words. No one ever got in his way. No one.

Especially this bebop on a bike. The avenging preppie.

Meanwhile, Frankie stared, speechless, at the figure who disappeared into the darkness beyond.

1

Morgan Hiller counted cockroaches. Lying on his bed, wrapped in the top sheet so that only part of his face was visible, he lay perfectly still, his eyes watchful, riveted, as two of the little beasts dodged each other among the chaos of unopened packing cartons, stacks of records and books, a busted track trophy, a pile of oxford shirts, and three pairs of sunglasses thrown on a once-handsome mahogany dresser. The roaches avoided his ten-speed bike, but when they crawled on his favorite poster of Albert Einstein, the little devils sounded their own death knell. Morgan lost control.

Like a cat, he crouched on his knees, ready

to spring into action, pulled two dart guns from under the top sheet, and zapped the roaches like a hero in a western movie.

He laughed wryly as he headed for the bathroom, pleased his day was starting out perfectly.

After a quick shower and shave, Morgan walked downstairs to the kitchen and heard his mother gabbing on the phone with her eldest son, Brian. Brian was the son who never gave his mother a hard time, never invoked the silent treatment, and always got good grades. He was even going to be a lawyer.

Although Morgan accepted the contrast between himself and Brian, he knew his mother couldn't. Mrs. Hiller could always cope with Brian, but she couldn't comprehend the complicated moods of her younger son. Actually, Morgan realized his mother couldn't deal with anything more complex than who to entertain at which party, what to serve for dinner, and which silk blouse coordinated well with each pair of trousers.

In a way, Mrs. Hiller's helplessness made her son feel sorry for her. Morgan knew she hated moving from their wonderfully luxurious house in Connecticut with its neatly trimmed lawns to the run-down bungalow in Los Angeles. He knew Page Hiller had never envisioned herself unpacking china in a tacky neighborhood at the age of forty-five. After all, she had married an executive. Who could have known he'd lose his job and wind up driving a cab at night while his youngest son got expelled from one of the best prep schools in the country?

Page Hiller was not cut out for adversity.

"Well, of course I'm worried, Brian," she said, not realizing Morgan was just within earshot. "You know what he did with his last term, and, my God, what I hear about this new school is just awful. I'm sure the kids there will just reinforce his old attitudes . . ."

Morgan shook his head. His mother would never quit. What he couldn't understand was why she thought Brian could do anything to change things. Nothing her eldest son could say or do would transform Morgan into a proper young man who would miraculously enter medical, law, or dental school within the next twelve months, because Morgan didn't want Brian's world. He wanted his own, even though he wasn't quite sure what that was yet.

Quietly wheeling his ten-speed out the door, Morgan disappeared before his mom could start complaining. He hopped on his bike, mentally preparing himself for the ordeal that was school. He hated first days; they made his skin itch. Just as he was about to pedal away, his father's cab came bouncing into the driveway.

"Hey, hotshot!" David Hiller greeted his son. His face was marked with the scars of failure and lines of fatigue. Driving the night shift always left him pooped, no matter how much he tried to sleep in the daytime. Being a cabbie wasn't like sitting behind a desk making big deals.

"So . . . first day of school. You up for it?"

"Aren't I always?" Morgan replied. "It's just me versus the pussycats, you know," he replied, realizing sharks would have been a better word for the neighborhood kids he'd seen hanging out.

"Yeah," David said. "Go get 'em."

Morgan pedaled easily down the street, hoping his father wouldn't see the slash in the back of his leather jacket.

Lawson was a typical sprawled-out rundown high school that bore the traces of too many years of students, most of whom would hardly look back at the time spent there as the finest of their lives.

The parking lot looked as if a carnival had just arrived. Kids dragged their feet slowly toward the entrance, yelling at their friends. Ghetto-blasters filled the air with music for show-off break dancers. Boyfriends and girlfriends made out like there was no tomorrow, while others flirted on the outskirts. The important thing was to see and be seen.

The first bell rang. Dented lockers banged shut as Nick Hauser surveyed the schoolday chaos around him. He paced near his rust-colored Camaro in the parking lot as his gang lounged lazily around him.

Frankie perched on the car's hood, busily applying makeup. She'd already put on a ton, but more lipstick couldn't hurt. She peered through her shades into her compact's mirror. Love Goddess Red, the perfect match for her striped shirt. A necklace of chains wrapped around her throat matched the chain belt cinching her too-tight jeans. She knew she looked good. And she knew she flaunted her best assets.

She glanced to where Ronnie and Eddie were busy slobbering all over each other, and ignored Nick's frustrated pacing.

"Man," Nick muttered, "I swear, if I ever get my hands on the bebop"—he placed his hands around his throat—"I'm gonna fuckin'—"

Frankie snapped her lipstick shut. "Watch your mouth, Nick."

Nick managed to look chagrined for about half a second. He hated it when Frankie criticized him. She was his girl and she better not forget her place. She'd better keep her trap shut or he'd show her how to shut it.

Maybe.

"Hey, lust puppy," Frankie called to Ronnie.

"Lust puppy?" What a stupid thing to say. "Look who's talking," Nick said, pissed off.

"That isn't rude," Frankie defended herself. "It's a simple statement of fact. Right, Ron?"

Ronnie rearranged her pink T-shirt, her pink sweater tied around cropped jeans, and pink socks. "One can only hope," she said, both girls giggling as they started to walk away.

And then Nick saw the real bebop. He recognized him from the back of his leather jacket. It was the same jacket, same patch, same big diagonal slash across it that could only have been caused by a snapped-off car antenna.

"I don't believe it," Nick said. The Tuffs followed his gaze in unison, staring dumbfounded, before closing in around Nick.

Frankie stopped and turned to see what was going on, abruptly wishing she hadn't. It was *him.* Those eyes. That same look.

Frankie turned toward Nick and saw a completely different look on Nick's face. Nick was out for blood.

"Hold it," Nick said, watching Lawson's sorely abused—and useless—security guard cut off Morgan's path.

"No bikes allowed on campus," the guard blustered.

"So sorry," said Morgan jokingly. "Here I was hoping to take a quick ride through history."

A quick elbow from Frankie cut off Ronnie's giggle.

The guard mustered all his authority. "Go park it over on the racks. And *walk* it all the way to the building."

Morgan nodded, and as he started to wheel his bike away, he whirled around to point at the guard's gun. "Ever shoot anybody with that thing?"

The guard looked at his gun and then back at Morgan, who flashed a wide smile at him and sauntered off.

Eddie and Mickey started walking after Morgan.

"Hey. Chill out," Nick said to them; this was too good to be true. "I said *chill*, man." Nick put his arm around Frankie and hugged her in pure delight. "I think we're going to school today."

The school office was chaos, as usual. New kids tried to hide in corners. The regulars stood around waiting for hall passes and late slips, ready with feeble explanations as to why they needed them in the first place. Day one, and the bullshit was flying already.

For instance, there was Howard Packard, senior, whose excuses had gotten a little rusty after a whole summer of freedom.

The school secretary, wise to what was coming, played dumb just to get back in the swing of things. " 'Morning, Howard."

"Um, my mother says I can be outta biology class today onaccounta I got this cold in my nose an' they got a whole buncha chemicals make me sick smelling 'em."

The secretary busied herself with some paperwork. "Then have your mother take the class. We have to have a body sitting in your chair, Howard."

Howard had the feeling he wasn't hearing what he wanted to.

The secretary deigned to look at the poor twit. "You're late for class, Howard."

Day one, and aced already. Howard slunk past two of his classmates, Jimmy Parker and Feather Molino. They were whispering in the late-pass line, paying no attention at all to anyone else in the crowded office.

Half of Lawson's female population was in love with Jimmy Parker. Not only did he play drums in a rock-'n-roll band, but he looked the part. In a school full of slobs he looked almost too hip. Nothing bothered Jimmy, whose usual response was, "Hey, state of the arts."

Jimmy was all dressed up for the first day of school in his favorite screaming turquoise shirt with the Jetsons on it, and a well-worn pair of cuffed black 501s. Ms. Molino, on the other hand, cultivated the subtle approach. The girl was never without an earring that gave her the nickname, or a chiffon scarf knotted around her neck in a color that perfectly matched the feather earring. Feather claimed the whole point of the scarf was to keep from catching cold. To hide her hickeys was more like it. Sometimes if you've got it, you can't flaunt all of it at once.

Jimmy and Feather were talking about the strange kid wearing sunglasses inside who sat oblivious, hunched up on two chairs, engrossed in *Love's Labour's Lost.*

"Where's he from?" Jimmy asked.

"Who cares?" Feather said. "His ass is grass now."

Jimmy gave Morgan an intense once-over, then whispered again. "Lemme have your blade."

"Why? You'll never use it."

"Yeah? Well, maybe I wanna clean my teeth," Jimmy murmured. "So fork it over."

Feather glanced at the harassed secretary, then discreetly pulled a folded pearl-handled switch-blade from the depths of her bra and palmed it to Jimmy.

"Later," he said as their esteemed principal, Mr. Russell, a middle-aged man with a no-nonsense face, stepped out of his office and called in the new student. Morgan stood up and followed the man into his inner sanctum.

"You want to take those off?" Russell pointed at Morgan's shades. "I like to see who I'm talking to."

Morgan complied silently and sat down, his face carefully neutral and controlled.

Mr. Russell glanced at the book on Morgan's lap. "Shakespeare, huh?" He fished out a file from the messy stack on his desk. "Actually, I don't know why I'm surprised. Your records show a very strong aptitude for English and writing. Going to do anything with that this year?"

Morgan shrugged.

Mr. Russell put a hand to his ear in a sarcastic gesture. "Excuse me?"

"I don't know."

The principal nodded, then leaned forward intently, his elbows on his desk. "Look, Morgan, I'm not going to waste our time on a lot of useless rhetoric I know you've heard before. You had a good education at one of the best prep schools in the country, and why you threw it away is luckily none of my concern at this point. What I am concerned about is your present attitude, which is my way of saying that I won't tolerate any of your bullshit—including impromptu rock concerts scheduled in between classes—no matter how much it seems to amuse your classmates. I've got enough trouble at Lawson dealing with the real losers without wasting my energy on a good imitation. Understand?"

"Yes, sir."

"All right," Mr. Russell sighed. "You better hustle or you'll miss your first class."

As Morgan left, Russell leaned back in his chair and shook his head. "If I had that boy's potential, I'd be running the country by now." His secretary walked into the office with another pile of files for his desk.

Everyone in school knew that American history was the biggest bore of all. Mrs. Baldwin was showing yet another cliché-riddled movie about the Old West. The black-and-white frames flickered across the faces of the students in the classroom, giving Morgan a chance to read *The Tempest* for the fourteenth time.

"After the original pioneers settled the land, a new breed was born," the movie narrator droned. The sound of gunshots actually woke students up. "These men were known as the gunfighters, and they brought a new code of honor to the Old West."

Everyone in class showed their appreciation of the sacrifices of yore by snickering and making duck heads with their fingers in front of the screen.

Morgan looked up from his book just as the movie actors got ready to draw. The guns went off in a blaze of glory, but the soundtrack wasn't loud enough to cover the spine-tingling click of a switchblade that registered in Morgan's ear. Morgan felt the blade brush his cheek.

Oh, God, it couldn't be starting again. He hadn't even done anything.

"Whoa, state of the arts," Jimmy whispered.

Mrs. Baldwin peered across her desk. "Problems, Jimmy?"

"Oh no," he said aloud, then whispered frantically to Morgan, "I just can't get the stupid thing closed." He fumbled with the catch, then dropped the knife as a few classmates sitting in the close vicinity started to snicker.

Morgan took the knife, palming it shut efficiently, and held it out to Jimmy, who looked at him with impish embarrassment.

"Sorry, man," he whispered again. "I've never had it out of my pocket before."

"No shit," Morgan said amiably, very relieved. "You better learn how to handle it before you chop your balls off."

Jimmy smiled. He could be friends with this guy. He was definitely okay. Too bad he was in for it.

"No, I want you to have it."

Morgan froze. This had to mean something. "Why?"

"Because it's all over school about you and Nick Hauser."

"Who?"

No time for explanations. That stupid cow of a teacher chose that moment to stroll up and pick on Jimmy. Morgan discreetly slipped the blade into his jeans pocket.

"Something up, Mr. Parker?"

"Yeah," Jimmy replied, only slightly flustered. "I was just, um, telling this guy about this book I read . . . *The Call of the Wild*."

Mrs. Baldwin braced herself. The thought of Mr. Parker actually reading was too much of a trauma to contemplate.

"And what was your reaction to this once-in-a-lifetime experience?"

"Oh," Jimmy sighed. "I didn't understand it, but I liked the dog."

Several classmates laughed as the teacher shook her head ruefully and returned to the movie projector. Jimmy shrugged and mouthed the word "later" to Morgan, who nodded.

Something was up. And Morgan had the sharp sinking feeling he knew what it was.

"Bebop a lu la," Morgan sang to himself as the narrator droned on. ". . . *Bat Masterson*,

Wyatt Earp . . . men who were made mythic by
their brutal pursuit of justice in a land that
had none . . ."

The only good thing about school was leaving it, Morgan thought as he and Jimmy left the
building together. They had met after the last
class and Jimmy was filling Morgan in on the
gang Morgan had angered the previous night.

"Wanna come to my gig tonight?" Jimmy
asked. "It's at this club called the Warehouse.
Just follow the porno shops east and you can't
miss it. I'll leave your name at the door."

Morgan truly laughed for the first time that
day. Jimmy was all right. Then he sobered up.
"Tell me about the Hausers."

"They're crazy, all of them. The whole family is legendary, man. Father's been in the
slammer. You name it, they've done it. And I
know. My brother Donnie used to be in a gang
with Nick's older brothers and it was total ter-
ror from the word go."

"They ever kill anybody?"

"No, but they sure made a few people suffer.
And I mean pain. You know?"

"Yeah." Morgan stopped. And that sharp sinking feeling became reality. He started across
the parking lot, his mouth set in grim deter-
mination. "I know."

Nick Hauser's mocking voice floated from the lot, above the noise of the gunning engines. "Bebop a lu la . . ."

Frankie's voice joined Nick's, singing the next line.

The two were helping themselves to a ride on Morgan's ten-speed. Frankie perched on front. Three cars circled them, each driven by a member of Nick's gang. A circle of students stood around watching, some silent, others laughing nervously.

Nick's Camaro raced right up to Nick and Frankie, but Nick didn't seem to care, or even notice. He kept right on singing. "Bebop a lu la . . . *now!*" Frankie screamed.

The Camaro's brakes squealed as the car gently nudged the back rim of the bike. Frankie laughed, taunting.

Morgan moved on instinct. He was tense, but walked purposefully to face the fools on his bike.

Jimmy tried to stop him. "Wait up!" He reached for Morgan's arm, but it was too late. "They're going to—listen! You're not listening."

Morgan wasn't listening.

The crowd grew larger.

"Just takin' it for a little test run," Nick sneered when he caught sight of Morgan.

"Yeah," Frankie shouted with a wide smile. "We want to make sure it's safe!"

In silence, Morgan continued toward his bike.
The engine of a Chevy revved up and the car
began to barrel down on him. As it drew nearer,
Morgan glanced at the Tuff who was driving it,
and with an unchanging expression, casually
dodged to the side as the Chevy swerved away.

"Hey, close," Nick shouted.

"But no cigar," Frankie added, her voice
fluttering. She was beginning to get a real knot
in her stomach. Was that guy looking at her
again? Like last night?

The crowd laughed nervously.

Jimmy watched Morgan in disbelief. "Death
wish," he said aloud. "The guy has a damn
death wish."

Frankie tried to hide her knot of nerves under a seductive smile. A Mustang shot out of
nowhere and aimed for the open space between
Nick and Morgan. As the car passed, Mickey
leaned out the window and sprayed red paint
in Morgan's face. "Rain from heaven!" he yelled,
then collapsed with laughter.

Morgan grimaced, then slowly took off his
shades and wiped them clean.

"Yo!" Mickey shouted. "I think he's got the
measles or something!"

Red speckles of spray paint dotted Morgan's
forehead and cheeks. Morgan squinted into the
sunlight and began walking calmly over to claim
his property.

"No, that wasn't fair," Nick said.

Frankie nodded nervously. "So . . . what do you think? Should we let him have it?" She could manage to bluff it out as long as the preppie didn't look at her, but he kept looking at her.

"Oh, absolutely," Nick replied.

Frankie was still perched on the new kid's bike. The Tuffs were shouting, egging them on, but all Frankie saw was that blue blaze of anger in the preppie's eyes. He was looking at her like Nick had never looked at her, and his stare made her flesh tingle. What did he want? Why did his glare affect her like this?

"Shit," Nick said. "What a jerk." He gave his girl a nudge and Frankie hopped off the bike, her eyes still glued to Morgan. Nick let the bike fall.

Morgan stood his ground silently, wondering what that girl saw in this maniac, knowing as he wondered that he'd pay for every ounce of his curiosity.

Why, on his first day in this dump of a school, was he already involved in a confrontation he hadn't provoked? Or *had* he? Morgan silently asked himself why he'd bothered to get involved in their petty thievery the night before. The guy at the bus stop didn't mean anything to him.

Wiping the paint from his mouth, Morgan replaced his sunglasses and reached down to pick up his bike. The crowd milled around in terrified silence. Time seemed to have frozen. In the distance, Morgan heard the muffled thunk of football players being tackled in the field. And then someone started a car and suddenly the Camaro was screeching across the asphalt, bearing down on Morgan Hiller.

At the very last second, Morgan jumped away from his bike and watched in horror as the car smashed into his ten-speed, hurling it high in the air, sunlight glistening off its spinning spokes. It hit the ground with a crash.

Nick walked up to Morgan and whispered in his ear, "Hey, I guess training's over, man. So sorry." Nick turned to the Tuffs. "You guys are bad," he told them, then laughed. "Nice bike— least it used to be."

Morgan turned to face Frankie. She felt the knot in her stomach dissolve into threads of guilt. She was confused and she couldn't look at Morgan anymore. She just wanted him to move back to wherever the hell in preppie land he'd come from.

"He said he was sorry," she said to Morgan, but she knew it wasn't enough. She ran after her boyfriend.

Jimmy came up beside Morgan and touched

the bike's twisted frame. They both glared at Nick walking away.

"Life is a bitch," Nick shouted from across the parking lot.

Yeah. Things were certainly going to be tough around here, Morgan thought to himself. But life was going to get harder for Nick Hauser, too.

2

Back in the privacy of his own room, Morgan checked out the damage to his bike. Usually Billie Holiday calmed him down, but not even "God Bless the Child" could soothe Morgan's nerves as he struggled to repair his bike.

"Shit," he said in complete frustration.

His mother chose that moment to knock on his door. She had an uncanny sense of timing—and it was always the *wrong* timing.

Uninvited, she barged into his room.

"Hi, honey. How was the first day?"

"Okay," Morgan said tensely. He dropped the wheel rim.

"Okay?" his mother persisted. "What happened to your bike?"

"Nothing."

"Nothing?" The familiar panicky edge started to fill her voice. "Your bike is in pieces and you say nothing? Morgan, if you're starting in again with the wrong crowd—"

"I'm not starting in again," he cut her off. "It was an accident, all right?"

Page couldn't deal with trouble again. "No, it's not all right. Who's paying for it? Did you find out if they have insurance?"

Morgan tried to keep his voice down, but he just couldn't ignore her nagging. He lost his cool in two seconds flat. "Mom, this isn't Connecticut. No one has insurance around here."

Page opened her mouth for a rebuttal, but her husband spared her the scene by stumbling into the room. "What's going on in here?"

"Your son said somebody ran over his bike."

David looked at Morgan. "Can you fix it?"

"Yeah. As soon as I learn how to walk on water, I'll get right to it," Morgan answered sarcastically.

Page exploded. "Don't take that tone with your father, young man. That was a five-hundred-dollar bike!"

"No shit!"

"I can't . . . I won't . . . I just won't deal with him if it's starting again." Page slammed her way out of the room.

David eyed his son. He knew Morgan's anger and pride had made him sound like a petulant child. Something had happened at school today, but David wasn't going to push the issue. Morgan would tell him about it in his own time, if he wanted to. David just had to give him a chance.

Morgan looked at his father. "Well, what do you expect me to say? I've been working on the stupid thing for hours," he said, hoping his father would understand.

"I expect you to try to understand her, Morgan."

The usual try-to-understand-your-mother routine. Why couldn't his father ask his mother to try to understand her youngest son?

Morgan picked up his jacket with a sigh and headed for the door.

"Dad," he said, glancing back, "I've been working on that one all my life." Morgan walked out, determined to find the Warehouse and let Jimmy's music obliterate the day's fiasco.

Sleazy was the only word to describe Van Nuys Boulevard. This city was the pits, Morgan said to himself as he kicked an empty beer can and stuck out his thumb, hoping for a ride. No luck, but that wasn't unusual these days. Hardly anything worked out for Morgan Hiller, and he wondered if anything ever would.

Turning around, he resigned himself to walking, cursing his bad fortune once more, wishing for his bike.

The sight of a gleaming black Porsche convertible parked in a no-parking zone outside one of L.A.'s finest sex shops caught Morgan's eye. He ran an appreciative hand over the slick dark frame, paused to check out the dash, and then stopped in total astonishment when he saw the keys dangling in the ignition. Opportunities like this only happened in the movies, he thought mischievously.

He quickly glanced around; then, not really knowing why, he took the keys and slipped them into his pocket. He'd return the car later, but first he'd give whatever dumb sex maniac had left them a scare he wouldn't forget easily.

Morgan found the Warehouse and went inside. The place looked like a meat market as prime-quality and fatback porkers danced to the beat. Morgan scanned the joint for some tenderloin, but only met vacant stares. God, these girls have no guts, no meat to them, he thought.

Yet he had to admit that the Warehouse had style. There was a wraparound balcony on the upper level, perfect for hiding couples who found dancing to be just the stimulant their mothers warned them against. The only adorning fixtures were haphazard hangings of huge old billboard advertisements. "Enjoy!" one of them proclaimed. San Diego ZT Dealer and Ringling Brothers Circus slogans were plastered on two other walls.

The circus down below moved en masse to the band on stage.

"It's too late," Jim Carroll sang, his hand gripping the mike.

Jimmy kept the beat steady with his drums and it was obvious that he loved sweating on stage. In fact, Morgan quickly realized, Jimmy loved being on stage, period. Morgan grinned. His new friend was okay.

Jimmy saw Morgan down in the crowd, and for a moment the two connected. Jimmy's shirt had long ago been discarded and he'd even managed to sweat through his black and red bondage trousers—English imports with all the buckles. He knew his outfit drove the girls crazy.

And the girls were going crazy. They had all spent hours fixing their hair, choosing their makeup, and producing their ultimate look. Feather's dangling trademark was blue tonight, matching the scarf around her neck. If her pants were any tighter she'd have to unglue them.

Ronnie had decided to go for the sex-tiger look, so she was dressed in yellow and black: a yellow T, black-and-yellow skirt, black heels, lace stockings—because everyone knew lace was happening—and a yellow scarf around her wrist. She twisted the scarf nervously as she gazed at Jimmy. He made her all crazy inside, but yellow gave her courage. She was a Leo, and Leos *had* to have courage. Maybe tonight she'd make her move, so Jimmy would know she was alive.

"Please, God, if you're up there, just let Jimmy see me," Ronnie implored.

Feather laughed. "Come on, Ronnie. Jimmy isn't your type."

"Yeah," Frankie added. She fitted perfectly into her clingy gray sweater dress, and as usual, looked stunning. She examined her nail polish: Devil-May-Care Red. It matched her shoes. Then she smoothed her fingerless lace mitts. Lace was definitely happening. "What about Eddie?" she asked Ronnie.

"Not the marrying kind, you know?" Ronnie replied, her eyes still glued on Jimmy.

Feather snickered and parked herself next to a couple of eligible bachelors nearby.

Ronnie dared to step closer to the stage. "Pain in my heart." She clasped her hands dramatically. "Come on, Frankie."

"No, I wanna wait for Nick."

"Oh, he'll find you." Ronnie turned to Feather. "You coming?"

"No," Feather purred. "I'm gonna stay right here and party, thanks."

Ronnie turned back to Feather, but her friend had already melted into the crowd. "Hypocrite," Ronnie said. "Fine, go ahead and dump me here." She stared at Jimmy, his chest glistening in the lights. Pain in her heart.

Frankie walked closer to the stage. She wanted to be by herself for a moment. Away from her best girlfriend and far away from Nick. She felt restless. She dodged her way through the dancers who were starting to form into two lines for the Warehouse version of the Stroll.

She didn't want to even admit to it to herself, but she was looking for something . . . someone.

And then she saw him. Bebop.

He was standing near the stage, smiling at Jimmy, when he suddenly turned his head. He saw her and his eyes widened.

Frankie felt lost. She panicked, turned, and elbowed her way through the crowd.

But Morgan was faster.

He grabbed her arm and she yanked it away. Her heart was racing. He reached for her again, and this time the snaking line of kids threw her right into his arms. She couldn't move and he wouldn't let her go.

They were dancing together before she even had a chance to protest. She tried to look around the dance floor for Nick, but there were too many bodies pressing up against them, forcing them to be together, and bebop's blue eyes looked straight into hers.

"Let go of me." Finally she had found her voice.

"Not until you tell me what your problem is."

"That's my business."

"Not anymore."

What did he mean—not anymore. Who did he think he was, anyway?

He eased her into a turn. She responded instinctively.

The beat went on.

Jim Carroll looked at his guitar player and smiled. "It's too late," he repeated, and the guitarist leaned into his instrument as the kids danced wildly all around the stage.

Jimmy couldn't believe what he saw. He half-stood up, but sat back down and fiercely crashed the high-hat. Morgan Hiller was just plain crazy or totally stupid. Or both. And it was going to get a lot worse because Nick Hauser, henchmen at his sides, had just sauntered into the Warehouse.

Nick was in a good mood that night, and he felt physical, like moving around. He didn't even bother to look for Frankie. He knew she'd be there, and she was probably beginning to wonder if he was gonna show. Well, let her sweat it out. She could wait.

Mickey cased the place. Finally he saw what he knew he shouldn't be seeing. Son of a bitch had really pushed his luck this time.

"Yo, Nick," he called. "Check it out, man."

Nick didn't hear him. He was into the beat.

"Hey," Mickey said, louder. "Nick. Talk about balls."

"What is it?" Nick asked. What was Mickey pestering him with now? Nick wanted to hear the song, to look at the bodies dancing, to chill out.

But then Nick looked. He blinked. It was the last thing he expected. It wasn't balls, it was a threat, a dare, a glove thrown down. This meant war.

Nick's eyes narrowed to slits as he regarded his Tuffs with disgust. What were they waiting for? "Go on!"

Nobody, but nobody, danced with his girl and got away with it.

Mickey and Eddie moved quickly onto the packed dance floor, elbowing their way through the crowd.

Frankie was halfheartedly struggling to escape Morgan's grip, but he moved too well and she was excited by this kid's energy. He twirled her, and she almost felt dizzy. Was it the turn or Morgan? She was being betrayed by her own body, her own curiosity. She couldn't understand why he was after her, or why she wanted him to be.

Morgan leaned her into a deep dip.

"You fool, you don't understand," Frankie

said in real desperation. She knew Nick had to be there by now. He'd kill Morgan, and he'd kill her too.

Morgan lifted her up, even closer, and Frankie thought he was going to kiss her. He held her so tight she couldn't breathe, but she didn't want him to let go. He couldn't let her go now—not when she was just beginning to admit to herself just how much she wanted him.

"It's too late," Jim Carroll sang.

Were those words for me? Morgan thought. Or were they for us both?

Mickey tried to push his way quickly through the dancers, but they shoved him back. He had to dance or get off the floor. Angrily he shoved his way through the gyrating bodies and moved in closer.

Frankie saw Mickey first and she caught her breath in fear.

Morgan saw her reaction, whirled her around, then let her go. She hurried off the floor, praying that Nick hadn't seen her. Then Morgan grabbed Mickey as he approached, and in a dancer's embrace, twirled him around, knocking him down into the crowd.

Jimmy stood up behind his drums. He'd seen nearly everything from the stage, and without realizing what he was doing, he'd sped up the pace, a staccato rhythm to match the pounding of his heart. Morgan was certifiable, of that he was sure. And he knew Hauser was a maniac.

The rest of the players in the band looked at the drummer in surprise. Was he on speed or what? their eyes seemed to ask.

Morgan melted into the crowd.

Nick paced furiously, scanning the dancers for that stupid bebop.

Ronnie stood nearby, nervously fidgeting with her yellow scarf. It didn't look like a good night for Leos.

Frankie staggered out of the crowd and Nick grabbed her roughly. "Take her home, Ronnie," he yelled. "Move it! The dance is over! I'll deal with you later," he told Frankie.

Nick's eyes were shooting sparks and Frankie split in a hurry. But she kept seeing Morgan's blue eyes flashing something entirely different, and she couldn't help but wonder what they held for her. She also was afraid to find out.

Morgan, sensing a confrontation he was too tired to deal with, left the Warehouse and tried to flag down a departing carload of kids. They didn't see him, though, as they took off into the night. He suddenly remembered the keys to the Porsche.

He hurried to the car when he felt someone watching him. He looked to the left: two Tuffs. He looked to the right: two more.

Nearly running, he'd just reached the Porsche when Mickey and Eddie grabbed him from behind. They shoved him up against a wall.

Nick came sauntering up and faced him. "I should just ace you now, scumbag."

"Why? Because I danced with one of your boyfriends?" Morgan said, glancing at Mickey. He knew his acerbic wit was not appreciated.

Nick actually paused, speechless. No one ever talked back to him like that. He couldn't figure out what was up with this asshole. Was he begging to get iced? At the same time, Nick forced down a surprising feeling of grudging respect for the guy's balls. Then he remembered Morgan had been dancing with his girl.

Tuff luck.

Nick suddenly had a brilliant idea. He looked at the Porsche. "This is a bad car, man. And you *owe* me." His eyes narrowed. "Enough of this bullshit. Give me the keys."

Morgan gave him the keys.

"Payment for services rendered, Hiller." Nick edged even closer. "And if you ever go near Frankie again, I'll take you out so fast you won't have time to spit."

With that he kneed Morgan viciously right where it hurt the most. Doubled in agony, Morgan fell as Mickey and Eddie hopped in the car and the black machine roared away.

Jimmy, drumsticks in hand, came running out of the club in time to hear tires squealing. "He took your car?"

Morgan could barely manage a smile. "I don't *own* a car, man."

That kid was too fresh for words, Nick thought as he sped down the boulevard. Mickey and Eddie sat in the back, laughing.

"Man," Mickey said, "this is just like in the movies."

When Nick pulled out the car stereo, they heard the siren.

"Shit," Mickey said, his voice rising.

"*Take* this," Nick said urgently, handing over the stereo with his right hand.

"Hey," said Eddie, "this is the first place they're gonna look."

"Nick. What are you gonna tell 'em. *Nick?*" Mickey asked in a panic.

"Shit," Nick Hauser said as he pulled over. He smacked the steering wheel with his fist. What the hell was he gonna tell 'em?

Another day at school had ended and Morgan couldn't help but feel it had been another waste of time.

He said good-bye to Jimmy and walked over to his locker. Something about it looked different. He reached out to touch it. Then he saw Frankie approach him.

She had been waiting for him, but now she

was a bundle of nerves. Morgan Hiller made her insides burn. Every time she saw him he made her completely forget about Nick, but she'd have to tough it out now.

"You may be smart, Hiller, but you're dead meat when Nick gets out of jail. He won't forget the car trick."

Morgan smiled calmly, but he remembered the price he'd had to pay for a dance. "And here I thought you were going out with such a nice respectable guy."

Frankie opened her mouth to retort, but found no words. She had no idea how to handle this guy. He was standing too close. If he touched her, she'd die. She hurried away.

Morgan opened his locker and froze. A dead rat was hanging from the top hook, its blood dripping all over his books.

Morgan grimaced in disgust. All his books, even his well-thumbed Shakespeare, were totally ruined.

He reached in his pocket for the switchblade and cut the rat free. He threw it into a nearby trash can, remembering the pet rat he and Brian had brought home, much to their mother's dismay, years ago.

But that was back in the days when Morgan and Brian were inseparable. Things had sure changed between them since then, and Morgan didn't particularly look forward to seeing his brother, who was coming home from school for the weekend.

Golden Boy would be full of witty advice for his younger, less fortunate brother, and Morgan didn't feel like dealing with Brian's attitude. It had been a hard week.

3

Brian Hiller always did what he said he was going to do. He was straight, dependable, and the apple of Mom's eye. Everything came easily for him, while everything seemed to be a struggle for his younger brother. Morgan had always felt intimidated by Brian's seemingly effortless success, his wholesome good looks, his charming facade, and the way he had swallowed the preppie vision whole. But lately, Morgan felt that Brian's cloning only made him a total fool.

Brian knew his brother was jealous, tense, and frustrated. Although Brian thought he tried to reach through to Morgan, he couldn't. It was easier to please his mother than to connect with Morgan.

So Brian sat outside and delivered his mono-logue as his mother cackled with appreciative laughter.

"Oh, go on," Page said. "Tell me some more."

Brian took a sip of wine. Rotgut California, he thought, but swallowed and smiled none-theless.

Page was overdressed, as usual, in a silk shirt, expensive and tailored pants more suitable for a country club than her new neighborhood.

"So there I was, in front of the entire review board, shaking like a total idiot. In fact, it got so bad at one point I thought I was going to rattle right off the platform."

"Doesn't matter," Page said proudly. "You still finished fourth in your class. It won't be long before you're the best lawyer in the country."

"Oh, Mom, I wouldn't go that far." Brian and his mother exchanged grins just as Morgan strolled outside.

"Hey, Golden Boy," he said to Brian. "How goes it?"

Brian tried to act nonchalant. "All right. You?"

"Okay." He sized Brian up in a glance, a vision in whiter shades of pale cream sweater, pale-yellow shirt, white pants (spotless, no doubt), white tennies (Jimmy Connors, no doubt). Bland. Typical. "So, you here for the weekend?"

"More or less." He knew what was coming.

"Then how 'bout letting me borrow your trusty BMW tonight?" It *was* Friday night, after all.

Page's mouth tightened as Brian tried to worm out of it.

"Well, I don't know, Morgan. I was thinking of taking Mom to the movies. You know, till Dad gets home."

Morgan tried to nail him. "I won't be gone long, Brian."

"I know." Brian squirmed. "And under other circumstances I'd let you have it in a shot, but we're probably leaving soon, so—"

"Forget it." Morgan cut him off and headed down the driveway.

"Morgan?" Page called.

Morgan had a shitload of nerve, Brian thought as he got up. "I'll handle it." This happened every time he came home. He ran out and caught up with his brother, grabbing his arm. "Why don't you cool out and give Mom a break?"

"Just as soon as she gives me one."

"Yeah? Well, she did, and look what you did with it."

"Just what's that supposed to mean?"

"That you cause trouble no matter where you are. And they spent a fortune to send you to decent schools and all you could do was screw up."

Morgan stared his brother down. There was— never had been—any way to get through to this vision in white. And he sure wasn't going to plead his case now.

"Brian, I'm *real* sorry. But I never wanted to go to those goddamned schools in the first place."

Morgan walked down the street, his fists shoved into his jacket pockets. Nothing he ever did was right, he thought through his rage. Only Golden Boy knew it all. From the moment he was born, Morgan had been programmed like his big brother. Only there was some glitch in son number two. And Mom sure didn't know what to do about it.

Neither did Morgan. Sometimes he wondered why he was so different, but most of the time he was just glad that he was.

He walked over to a bench at a bus stop and sat, fidgeting. Sometimes, in a fit of melodramatic self-pity, he thought of Pigpen in the *Peanuts* cartoon, who always had a cloud of dirt tracking him. Morgan knew he always had a cloud of trouble trailing his steps.

He moped some more. Did he really need, he asked himself over and over, attention all that badly? Was that why he was so different? He didn't see the rust-colored Camaro cruise by at first. But the driver saw him and, screeching to a stop, made a quick U-turn.

The roar of the engine woke Morgan from his reverie. When he saw that car he knew he had to get away. He hopped over the bench and began running for his life.

He dodged into an alley, hurling back garbage cans as the Camaro closed in on him.

Dead end.

Morgan scaled a chain-link fence, but there was barbed wire on top. He was fenced in.

The car kept coming.

Morgan fell to the ground, his chest heaving. He pulled out the switchblade and snapped it open, waiting for the inevitable. It seemed like hours before the car door opened.

Morgan heard the handle, then the click, then the crunch of a shoe on gravel. An apparition appeared. It had Jimmy's face. Jimmy's laughing face . . .

"Some fucking joke!" Morgan yelled, releasing the tension that had built up within. "What are you doing with Nick's car?" he asked.

Jimmy looked nonchalant. "Hey! *His* brother called and asked *my* brother to pick it up. Donnie wasn't home, so here I am!" He offered Morgan his hand. "Come on, I'll give you a ride in your favorite car."

Morgan stood up. What a maniac.

Jimmy gave him the once-over. "Pretty tough
. . . your jeans are still dry."

The guy was hopeless. Morgan smiled and
snatched the keys from Jimmy's fist. "I wanna
drive."

"Don't you trust my driving expertise?"

Morgan shoved him in the Camaro.

Everyone hung out at the Drive-In for grease-
burgers. The outside tables were a perfect van-
tage point for gossips, and the waitresses ignored
just about all the disgusting behavior around
them.

Ronnie and Feather were discussing Lawson's
favorite new subject, Morgan Hiller. Frankie
pretended to look bored as she spun the straw
in her Diet Coke and clinked the ice cubes
together.

"I dunno," Feather said as she ate a french
fry, leaving a faint smear of ketchup on her
pink lower lip. Today she featured black. "If
you ask me, he's either the toughest guy who
ever came to Lawson or the stupidest."

Ronnie, her mouth full, answered. "No way.
He went to one of those awesome brain facto-
ries back East"—she pointed a crimson nail at
her skull—"and I mean the guy's head is totally crammed, you know?"

Frankie stuck in her two cents. "Yeah,
crammed with bullshit."

"Whatsa matter with her?" Feather asked.

"Pining cuz Nick's still in the slammer." Ronnie grinned. "You know how she gets when she isn't getting any."

Feather ignored Frankie's glaring pout. "Yeah, well, if you ask me, she's hot for you know who. I saw those two dancing the other night. Body heat on contact—and I mean sizzling." She sucked in another fry.

Ronnie giggled.

"Cram it," Frankie said, standing up. She dealt with her problems by ignoring them and hoping they would go away. But she had the feeling—worrying and thrilling—that Morgan Hiller was a problem that was not going to go away.

"Let's go, Ron. The air's getting a little thick around here."

"But I'm not finished."

So Frankie really crammed it, and smashed the burger in her best friend's face. "You are now!"

Dumbfounded, Ronnie sat staring at Feather as mustard inched down her neck. Feather thought it was the funniest thing she'd ever seen.

As Morgan cruised, Jimmy examined Nick's tape collection with disgust. "How could anyone listen to this shit?" he said. "No wonder

Hauser acts the way he does—he's rotted his brain." Jimmy chucked a tape out the window.

"Put on the radio, at least. Nothing here to listen to."

"Breakin' the Rules" blared.

"I just don't know what it is," Morgan continued explaining, "but it's always been like that. If I didn't follow big brother's lead, it was like I was invisible."

"Same with me and Donnie." Jimmy nodded in agreement. Another cassette hit the dust. "The only reason I didn't have to join a gang was because he got his ass kicked so bad my mom outlawed the shit." He pulled out another tape. "Aha! This is Nick's favorite." He tossed it. Nick would never appreciate the favor Jimmy had done for him.

"What happens if you break tradition?"

"Don't know and don't want to find out."

They smiled as Morgan drove on. He knew what he was looking for but had no hope of finding it. When he saw Frankie on the sidewalk near the Drive-In, he thought, at first, that it was some conjured-up vision, some imaginary figure of wish fulfillment. But the apparition was alive. It tapped its toe impatiently on the sidewalk and looked pissed off.

When Morgan swerved over, Jimmy looked up to see why. No way. He tried to grab the wheel. "No way, man! She's trouble. She's Nick's."

"All I want to do is talk to her."

"And all I want to do is live!"

Morgan laughed and leaned on the horn.

Frankie didn't hear it at first. She was too busy feeling ashamed of herself. Ronnie hadn't deserved that, but every mention of that stupid Morgan Hiller drove her apeshit. Men were so confusing, she thought. But at least she always knew where she stood with Nick.

Ronnie finally appeared, trying to wipe off the damage. She looked around, brushing hamburger juice off her lucky-charm necklace, thinking Frankie was a pain sometimes, and then she stuck her hand down beneath her black-and-white layered T and pulled out a piece of bun. She glanced down at her transparent baby-blue petticoat which was her pride and joy, and heaved a huge sigh of relief. If that had gotten messed, she would have died.

Frankie turned when she heard the horn. A wide smile flashed on her face. "I don't believe it! Nick's out!" She turned back to Ronnie. "Come on . . ."

"Get in the back," Morgan ordered Jimmy as the girls approached.

"Forget it, chump!"

Morgan started to haul him over. They were both laughing.

Jimmy gave in. "Okay, okay, I'll get in the back."

As he clambered over, Frankie yanked the door open and leapt into Morgan's arms. Then she looked. *"You?"*

Morgan smiled. Ronnie hurried in, not even looking, and crawled in the back.

Morgan floored it and the burst of speed threw Ronnie right into Jimmy. Heaven, she'd died and gone to heaven. Someone up there loved her after all.

"Thank you, God!"

The Camaro eased into freeway traffic, heading for Beverly Hills. A bemused Jimmy was pretending to fight off Ronnie's groping paws as Morgan and Frankie battled it out up front. Although Ronnie was awfully cute Jimmy knew a guy couldn't be just an object of lust. But, he figured, maybe he could accommodate the ladies once in a while.

"But all I want to do is talk," Morgan said.

Frankie couldn't believe this was happening to her. She wasn't ready for this. She knew Nick would kill her. "And I just spent twenty minutes telling you I have nothing to say. So let me out!" she practically yelled.

Jimmy leaned forward. "Let her out, man."

"Not till we work this out." Morgan glared at his friend.

Ronnie grabbed Jimmy. "Work it out, Frankie. Go for it."

Frankie couldn't believe Ronnie would betray her too. Morgan Hiller certainly affected people strangely. "We have nothing to go for," Frankie spit out. "He blew it, and now he has to pay." She knew she had to be tough or she'd crack.

"Come on," Morgan said. "You don't mean that."

Jimmy sounded desperate. "Yes she does!" Jimmy wanted to live.

Ronnie sounded desperate too. "No she doesn't!" Ronnie wanted to live forever in the backseat with Jimmy.

Frankie and Morgan turned to look at their friends. "Will you two stay out out of this?" they said simultaneously. Surprised, they glanced at each other, then burst out laughing as Jimmy heaved a sigh of resignation and Ronnie heaved one of delight.

Embarrassed, Frankie looked at her nails.

Morgan took advantage of her obvious confusion. "Nice smile."

"Thanks," Frankie said. "But it still doesn't change anything between us."

"Oh, I don't know. I got a smile. Maybe if I wait long enough, I'll get lucky."

"Don't hold your breath." Frankie tried to look irritated. But she couldn't. This guy was turning her world inside out, and the worst part about it was she liked it. She liked him. And she didn't know what to do about it.

4

Morgan drove through Beverly Hills and every-one gawked in wonder at the surrounding estates. Protected by gates, shrubs, alarms, and computers, the ostentatious Beverly Hills man-sions looked more like movie sets than homes for real people. Morgan had seen it all before.

"Where are we?" Jimmy asked, and everyone stared at him. Any bozo knew it was where the movie stars lived. There was a big sign down the road. MOVIE STAR MAPS SOLD HERE.

"It's the other side of the moon," Morgan said.

Ronnie pointed at one extravagant estate. "No lie ... you could fit my entire apartment on their front porch."

"I wonder how many people live there," Frankie asked.

"Four and a half," Morgan deadpanned.

Ronnie giggled. "Who's the half?"

"No one knows. They're too embarrassed to let him out."

Morgan turned the corner and cruised past a wide expanse of green.

"Whoa," Jimmy said, pointing. "Check out that lawn. One perfect block of green."

"That's cuz it's a golf course," Morgan said.

"You sure?" Ronnie asked. "What a waste of space."

"Yeah. Unless it's become fashionable to plant flagpoles instead of roses." An idea hit him, and he drove into the parking lot of the golf course's country club.

"Tee-off time, huh?" Jimmy asked.

"No. We're going to eat."

Morgan's reply made Frankie get nervous. "Here? Like this?"

"That's right," he said. "They always have the best food on juniors night."

"How d'ya know it's juniors night?" Ronnie asked, not really sure she knew what that was anyway.

"Because it's Friday. And rich people run their children's lives on perfect schedules which coincide with what they want to do. The parents want to go out Friday night, and they need somewhere where they know their kids will be safe and mingle with the 'right' crowd."

Frankie didn't know what to make of this kid from Connecticut. She had assumed he *liked* his comfortable life back East, but Morgan definitely sounded bitter.

Morgan got out of the car, but Frankie held back a little. She didn't know why she felt so embarrassed. Just a short while before she'd been smashing burgers in Ronnie's face, but now she tugged at her skirt, and read the sign: WELCOME TO THE WEEKLY JUNIORS TOURNAMENT AND DANCE.

She looked at Morgan, who was checking out the clothes situation.

"We'll have to try to look a little respectable to get in," Morgan said.

Jimmy was, as usual, in one of his fave loudly printed shirts over an airbrushed T with the well-worn cuffed black denims and white socks. Morgan handed him a dark-blue shirt that had been in the car.

"Here . . . Jimmy," Morgan said, making him take off the shirt and put on the other one. "And slick back your hair. Great."

Jimmy wasn't quite country-club material, but it was all Morgan could do for him on such short notice.

Morgan turned to face Ronnie. He noticed her transparent baby-blue petticoat for the first

time. *Definitely* not country-club material. "God
. . . Ronnie."

"Pretty hopeless, huh?"

"No, God, no, Ronnie. Here." Suddenly Morgan had an idea. "Jimmy, give me your shirt. Ronnie, put it on and clinch it at the waist with your belt." It hid the worst and clashed wonderfully with her charm necklace. "Now fluff up your hair, get heavy on the eyeliner, and don't say anything but *fabulous* unless they put a gun to your head."

"Why not?"

"Because you just arrived from Europe and you can't say anything else." He stepped back and surveyed the transformation. "You're fantastic."

Ronnie wasn't used to compliments. She couldn't believe her luck. First the backseat, and now Jimmy's shirt on her back. I can die happy, she thought. And it's all because of Morgan, she realized, and suddenly Morgan wasn't as much of a jerk, after all, no matter what Nick or Eddie might have said. Then all thoughts of Eddie Baker flew out of her head. She smiled radiantly at Jimmy. Everything was *fabulous*.

Morgan turned to Frankie, who had been surveying the imposing clubhouse and the fleet of imported sports cars littering the parking lot. She wondered how much money it cost to live like this all the time. The parameters of her own life had been defined by her father's liquor shop, by the parking lot at Lawson High School, and lately by Nick Hauser. She'd never questioned any of it, but simply accepted the facts. That way she wouldn't know what she was missing. She was certain she would die before she acted like the stupid preppettes who turned into sappy Lawson cheerleaders.

She looked at Morgan and suddenly wondered if he had always gone out with Connecticut cheerleaders. Frankie couldn't imagine what a kid like him could see in a girl like her. Their images just didn't seem to mesh. Yet something inside of Frankie told her that Morgan had the guts *and* the brains to back it up. And she knew Nick wasn't overly endowed in the brain department. In fact, Frankie couldn't remember exactly what she saw in Nick Hauser besides the fact that he was familiar. She silently cursed Morgan Hiller for causing so much confusion inside her head.

At the same time, she accepted the white cotton sweater he had taken off and handed her.

"Put this on. It'll look great on you," he said.

Frankie pulled the sweater over her head and knew it was a perfect fit. It was oversized and trendy and looked made for her short black skirt and red high heels.

"Tie your hair up," Morgan instructed.

Frankie twisted her masses of golden hair into a loose knot and glanced at Morgan. He smiled and Frankie smiled back.

"Here." He handed her his shades. "Keep these on and look bored."

"That won't be hard," Ronnie said. "She's always bored."

Frankie glared at her friend and then they both laughed. This was going to be one fun evening.

Morgan tucked in his shirt, ran his fingers through his hair, and in the span of two seconds transformed himself. At that moment Morgan looked remarkably like his older brother. Maybe it was his posture or his coolly competent attitude. Whatever it was, it was there.

Morgan stuck his head into the back of a nearby Rolls, which, of course, was unlocked. "Fools!" he hissed, eyeing a tennis racquet in the backseat. He grabbed the perfect prop.

"C'mon," he said as he beckoned toward the clubhouse. "This is only good for about twenty minutes, so eat fast."

The clubhouse foyer smelled of money. Not old money, but nouveau money. Airy, spacious, with masses of flowers in vases adorning the filigreed tables, the entrance echoed with the mundane chitchat of well-bred future investment brokers who'd never heard of Lawson High School and thought the Warehouse was a place to store Daddy's little trinkets before they got shipped to the Third World, wherever that was.

Morgan burst in, Frankie's hand firmly in his, waving his racquet at everyone and no one. He acted like he owned the place. "Patty, Alan . . ." he called out. "How *are* you?"

Three couples turned and waved. Of course he looked familiar. Just what was his name?

"*Fabulous*," Ronnie said, clutching Jimmy's arm. "Fabulous!"

Morgan saw trouble approaching from across the room and it looked remarkably like an older version of Golden Boy. Clad in a raw-silk suit, with a yellow silk shirt and tie and cream-colored socks and shoes, the man had a super-cilious expression and a nametag that read REYNOLDS.

"Young man," Reynolds said to Morgan, his voice full of authority. Reynolds ruled the de-signer sweat set with an eagle eye. No interlop-ers on this turf, please. "I must see your membership card."

Morgan flashed his most charming smile and gestured with the racquet, quickly buying time to scan the man's nametag.

"Oh, Reynolds, I'm so sorry. I'm afraid I've

been a terrible fool and left it in my locker with my tennis rags."

Reynolds disdainfully surveyed the motley crew. "Then you'll just have to wait while I send someone for it."

Morgan realized that would give them all a chance for a quick snack. Turning to the three couples as they curiously approached the new-comers, he said carelessly, "Oh, I'm sure Patty and Alan will vouch for us."

The couples, not sure exactly who he was talking about, nodded like puppets. Morgan hurriedly pulled Frankie through the door into the main dining room.

It was almost too easy.

"*Fabulous!*" Ronnie screeched.

It was a typical Friday night for the juniors. They picked at the food on the expansive buffet, gossiped, and traded stock-market tips. More energetic souls danced to the halfhearted beat of a band grooving on the kind of version of "Twist and Shout" usually heard in elevators.

Jimmy stared at the band in disbelief. "Man, I don't know what they got, but I sure hope I don't catch it."

Morgan wouldn't let go of Frankie's hand. "C'mon." He tugged at her. "I'm starved."

Frankie held back. "I can't."

"Why not?"

She felt humiliated. "Because everyone's staring at me."

"That's because the girls are trying to figure out where they've seen you before, and the guys wanna know why they haven't. Either way, they're totally green with envy and will be fighting like cats when the night's over."

Frankie flashed Morgan a grateful smile and relaxed. The whole thing was too unreal for words and she didn't want to fight it anymore.

Jimmy turned to look for Ronnie and saw her edging over to the buffet. He was warming up to the situation even if the jerks dancing to this Muzak were mutants.

Nearly bumping into a clean-cut junior carrying an overloaded plate back to his table, Jimmy suddenly felt hungry. He helped himself to a canapé off the guy's plate and surveyed the mounds of food with disdain. "Honestly, poached salmon, again. How passé. I must have a word with the chef." He wiped his fingers on the guy's napkin. "Any time."

Now he needed something to wash the awful taste out of his mouth. He positioned himself next to a girl sitting alone.

"May I seet down . . . ex-kews me," he said in a terribly fake accent. "May I? Yes. Did anyone ever tell you that you have boo-teeful teeth? Yes? No? Are you an actress? You see"—he leaned toward her confidentially—"I come here

weet my father—he is over there somewhere—
and we are big Hollywood producers. Yes. We
come to work with Barry Manilow. You know
heem? We know heem very well. One of my
very best friends. Yes? You like to be in movies?"

The girl blushed.

Jimmy caught a glimpse of Reynolds. It was
time to chow down and split.

"Ex-kews me . . . I see my father waving . . ."

Ronnie swished her way past some tables on
her way to the food.

"Her hair looks like a rat's nest," one girl
said.

"That outfit is so tacky," another chimed in.

"I know I saw that skirt in Italian *Vogue* last
month."

Ronnie heard them. She stopped and turned
around, smoothing her skirt haughtily. "Dar-
leeng!" she gushed to the girl who had made
the crack about her hair. "Don't you know?
Pearls are out. *Charms* are in."

Smothering her laughter, Ronnie walked to
the dessert table. She figured a few truffles
never hurt a girl, and forgot her diet. As she
reached for a handful, she noticed a table of
guys staring at her. They all looked like turkeys!
She bit into a truffle slowly, watching the guys
the whole time, and then licked her lips and
blew the boys a wet kiss.

"*Fabulous!*"

Frankie was down at the other end, picking at the pâté. Ronnie joined her, looked at a canapé topped with black stuff, and took a bite. She spit it out.

"What is this slimy, salty stuff?" Ronnie asked. "Who wants to be rich if you have to like this kind of junk?"

Frankie picked up half a lobster. "I don't know, what's this?"

"Who cares?" Ronnie said as she saw Reynolds approach. "You'll never see it again."

Morgan also caught a glimpse of Reynolds. Though Morgan looked perfectly at ease in the opulent room, he still felt completely detached, less like one of these kids than Frankie or even Ronnie. It was like he was walking in a transparent bubble. They saw him clearly enough, but he was behind a self-imposed wall of isolation. And they'd never know it.

He overheard snatches of a conversation about commodities trading. "Stick to real estate," he interjected as he walked by. "Build equity. Why bother with brokers?"

He stopped to straighten one guy's tie. "Nice cravat. Halston gave me one just like it last year."

Morgan smiled and sauntered off. Two other guys were discussing college admissions. "Yeah, well, Dad had the president of his company write a recommendation letter for me for Harvard," the kid bragged.

"Well," Morgan said in passing, "that's nice, but I was lucky to have the president write mine."

Where was Frankie? He found her eyeing arugula and shiitake mushrooms with disgust.

Reynolds was staring at Jimmy's pocket with horror. There was a full-length baguette sticking out of it. Reynolds deftly appropriated his club's property. Just who were these interlopers anyway?

Jimmy tried to look sheepish.

Time for a little diversion, Morgan thought. "C'mon." He pulled Frankie across the dance floor.

The band looked happy and well-fed. Dressed in a jacket and bow tie, their lead singer surveyed the crowd. "Did you come in a BMW?" he crooned to a couple swaying on the off-beat. "I bet you did. I did once."

The song ended with a resounding thud on the high-hat and Jimmy winced.

"Okay, ladies and gents." The band leader smiled into the mike. "We're going to take a short break—"

"—and we're going to entertain you while they do," Morgan said as he grabbed the mike from the guy's hand and hoisted Frankie on top of the piano.

Bewildered, she tugged at her skirt.

Morgan tickled his fingers on the keys to loosen them up. "Can you sing?" he asked Frankie.

Her eyes widened. "NO! No way!"

He winked, "Just teasing."

Frankie looked around the room. Everyone was staring at her, but she didn't care anymore.

> I feel the thunder
> I feel the pain
> I know the struggles you keep
> The nights in the rain . . .

Morgan sang to her. She smiled, relaxed and enjoying every minute of Morgan's charade.

> I feel your face
> I hear your eyes
> I know the nights that you cried
> But still we survive . . .

Couples eased onto the dance floor and Frankie glanced at them, wondering if Morgan made them feel all mushy inside too. He scared her, but she liked him.

> I walk the night
> I walk the night
> Fighting the darkness that
> Breaks our hearts
> We hold each other tight.

Morgan felt like a man possessed. While he

sang his words, he was in control and nothing he did was wrong. He sang to Frankie, and for the moment the rest of the world ceased to exist. Nick Hauser was merely a fragment of a dream, and all he saw was this girl, her timid smile, her confusion.

He could be the one to make it right for her too, and it would be the best thing Morgan Hiller had ever done.

> I feel your tears
> I touch your smile
> We lick our wounds
> Till light rips through the night . . .

Without even thinking about it, Jimmy pulled Ronnie into his arms and they began to dance, though it was a bit awkward with bulging pockets of smoked turkey and cheesecake. "That Morgan Hiller is full of surprises," Jimmy whispered in Ronnie's ear.

They listened, swaying, until Jimmy spotted Reynolds oozing impatient paranoia at the other end of the dance floor.

Jimmy quickly eased Ronnie out of sight.

> We walk the night
> We walk the night
> Fighting the darkness that
> Breaks our hearts
> We hold each other tight
> We walk the night
> We walk the night.

Frankie (Kim Richards) and Morgan (James Spader).

Frankie in the parking lot of Lawson.

Nick Hauser (Paul Mones).

Morgan and Jimmy (Robert Downey) watching Frankie and Nick borrow his bike.

Confrontation in the parking lot.

Ronnie (Olivia Barash), Frankie, and Feather (Catya Sassoon) between classes.

Nick tries to apologize to a confused Frankie.

A surprise visit from Morgan.

Ronnie and Jimmy in the back seat.

Ronnie's first taste of caviar: "Who wants to be rich if you have to eat this stuff all the time?"

The final fight: "So, Bebop, how's the silver spoon feel now?"

Frankie dares to pull the trigger.

Applause filled the air, but Morgan didn't hear it. Frankie leaned down closer.

Reynolds broke the spell. He barged over, a quivering creampuff of righteous indignation. "You are *not*," he bellowed, his pointing finger trembling with anger, "nor have you *ever* been, a member of this club."

So much for the serenade.

Morgan tried not to laugh. "Well, how about that, Frankie!" He lifted her off the piano, and they both regarded Reynolds with disdainful hauteur for his effrontery.

Reynolds watched them leave, conflicting emotions sweeping over his face.

"Cheeky bastards," he muttered, trying to repress a smile. He would have done the same thing if he'd still been young.

5

In Beverly Hills, window shoppers still lined the street and lazy couples licked ice-cream cones.

Frankie and Morgan walked past fountains spraying mist into the evening air. Frankie suddenly realized she was alone with Morgan, and she felt as shy and uncertain as she had when they walked into the country club. This guy was definitely getting under her skin. With a jolt she realized she hadn't thought of Nick since she'd gotten into his Camaro. But she knew he'd pulverize her when he found her out.

Her steps faltered for a minute, but then she

felt the cool mist on her face, and the comforting sound of the cascading water soothed her nerves.

Morgan quietly watched the confusion flicker in Frankie's eyes. He didn't dare push his luck. This girl was too special to lose now.

"What about Ronnie and Jimmy?" Frankie asked.

"I've got the keys, remember? We'll probably find them in the backseat later."

Frankie smiled. The air was balmy, and tonight was like one of those nights she'd only heard about. Everything was more special, more memorable, more enchanted. And she felt safe.

For the moment.

"What did you mean when you sang that song?"

"Just what I said."

"It's funny . . . I mean," Frankie mumbled, not sure of what to say. "I never heard a guy admit anything like that before." She couldn't meet his eyes.

"You mean Nick never told you he needed you?" Morgan asked, hoping Frankie would say something. He had to know if she really loved Hauser.

Frankie ignored his statement.

"So were you really rich before you moved? Or is that just another one of Ronnie's famous rumors?"

Morgan laughed. "No, we were doing okay until my dad lost his business."

Their eyes met, then Frankie studied some cigarette butts on the sidewalk. "Will you go back? I mean, to college and stuff."

"I wasn't planning on it." He looked at her intently. "What about you? Going for the scholastic gold?"

"Are you kidding?" Frankie laughed sarcastically. "I'll be lucky if I graduate. No, I'll probably just get married. You don't need college for that."

"Your parents happy about that?"

"My dad is." Frankie looked at the water glistening in the dark. "My mom died of cancer last year."

"I'm sorry."

Frankie's eyes filled involuntarily with tears, and she reprimanded herself for being such a baby. She needed to chill out.

"So you feel like dancing?" she asked, trying to break the mood.

"Sure," Morgan said gently, thinking they had both joined the ranks of the walking wounded and feeling closer to Frankie than ever. He was sure Nick Hauser didn't deserve anyone as good as Frankie; the Tuff had no idea what he had.

Club 60s was the place to go for the well-heeled early-thirties crowd who could afford the exorbitant cover charge, and Frankie sweet-talked their way in. She knew just how to ca-jole a doorman. Morgan couldn't believe her rap.

The glitzy club was alive, and the floor rever-berated with the drummer's backbeat. Revolving globes threw jewel-colored patterns of light on the dancing bodies below. A sequined go-go girl let it rip in a cage on the side of the stage.

The band paused before launching into an-other number. Figures appeared behind a trans-parent screen, horns in hand, before leaping on stage. Jack Mack grabbed a mike. Lights flashed, bodies moved, and the sax wailed. "She's look-ing good."

Frankie felt all the tension leave her body. She was going to dance, and nothing else mattered.

Except Morgan. She pulled him on the dance floor with her.

It was too hot for his sweater. She pulled it off, and as she did, her hair fell from its knot. She felt the weight of it flash around her face as she started to move in rhythm to the beat, a woman possessed.

She was dancing with all her pent-up energy, for herself and for Morgan. It was a mating dance for an enchanted evening, and Frankie had center stage.

She whirled giddily, revolving like a moon

around Morgan, and he could only watch, bemused and a bit stunned, because he knew this was her dance and she was performing it for him.

Other couples screamed their appreciation and moved back to give her room.

Frankie danced across the floor, then leapt on a table, leaning over in a backbend. She moved like a gazelle from table to table, stopped at one to pick up a drink, and downed it with a flick of her wrist. Then to the customer's astonishment she slid down the table and touched earth once more.

She did a flip over to the bar, but that wasn't enough. She got on top of the bar and danced down its length. She ran over to the go-go cage, joined the dancer, and copied her movements, shimmying with the lights in her eyes and the sweat trickling down her back. She felt hot.

The band joined in as Jack Mack sang to her alone. "She's looking good . . ."

The crowd was going crazy; the girl was electrifying. She leapt down and danced over to Morgan. He reached out to touch her, but she was still doing a solo, flying high on her own energy.

Her body was a weapon and she had trained it well, for just this moment.

The crowd was screaming; the horns were alive.

Frankie twirled once more, danced on a chair, and heard the song's finale. She spotted Morgan, leaning up against a pillar, then threw herself into a cartwheel and landed in his arms. It was just where she wanted to be.

"Whoa!" Jack Mack said on stage, shaking his head. "Gettin' a little hot in here. Let's cool things down . . ."

Frankie pulled Morgan closer. She kissed him, passionately, her body energized, her desire unmistakable. Morgan returned the kiss. God, how he wanted her.

Confidently brazen, Frankie grabbed his hands and placed them on her breasts.

But Morgan froze. Not yet. Not here. He kissed her lightly, then pulled back for real.

"Frankie," he said gently. "No. I'm sorry. I don't know you well enough."

Frankie's ears were ringing from the music. She didn't want to hear what she thought she heard. "What's there to know?" she asked in bewildered indignation. "I'm a girl and you're a boy."

"More." He tenderly kissed the top of her head. "Much, much more." He turned to leave.

Frankie got the message. She felt like a fool. A crazy, bitchin' fool.

*   *   *

Croyden Liquors was usually quiet early in the morning. But this morning was different.

Nick Hauser was out of jail, and he was going out of his mind, yelling at Frankie at the top of his lungs. "What do you *mean* you *had* to go out with him?" he screamed.

"Just what I said!" she screamed back.

"Don't lie to me, Frankie."

He shook her violently. Her dresser mirror reflected his rage from three different angles.

"I'm not lying! Don't you ever lay hands on me like that again, or I swear you'll wish to God you'd never laid eyes on me."

Tears of rage, humiliation, and frustration filled her eyes as she turned away from the mirror. Away from the look in Nick's eyes. It wasn't like the look in Morgan's eyes at all.

Nick stood, actually feeling helpless for the first time in his life. He felt like he was losing something, but he didn't know how to say what it was. He didn't recognize this girl anymore. "I'm sorry, baby," he tried.

Frankie felt the tears form faster. Nick Hauser never apologized to her before. Nick Hauser never apologized to *anyone*.

"It's just made me a little crazy, that's all," he explained. "You know I need you—"

Need? Frankie remembered Morgan had asked her about need. And she hadn't answered him.

Everything was just too confusing for her right now.

"How do you think it makes me feel, knowing you were with him?" Nick persisted.

Frankie almost wished Nick would tell her how it felt because he never explained his feelings to her.

He came up behind her and put his arms around her.

She stiffened.

Nick pulled her around. "Hey—"

"I can't look at you." Frankie couldn't face his eyes.

"What do you mean, you can't look at me?" Nick was going to get that rotten bastard Morgan Hiller for doing this to him.

"Not now," Frankie said.

"Not now?" He kissed her, easing her down on the bed. "What's the matter, baby?"

Frankie couldn't fight anymore; she couldn't even think. She wanted to sleep, to be left alone. How could she hope to explain what she didn't understand herself?

"Don't be so rough. We don't do it unless I say it's okay, remember?"

Nick was so easy. She was used to him and he didn't ask her questions.

Nick smiled. He'd won this one. "I thought you liked it rough."

"Not now, okay?"

She was his. He tried to be gentle, kissing her lightly on her cheeks, her neck, her body, her hair. Her hair smelled wonderful.

Frankie turned her head away, her eyes shining with tears.

6

Thirty-five guys hit the locker room at the same time screaming and yelling. Someone turned on a radio.

"Hey, turn it up," Morgan yelled to the owner of the ghetto-blaster.

"This place stinks," said the tall skinny guy whose locker was next to Morgan's, throwing his running shoes into the back of his locker.

"Yeah, I hear you. It's just the air's stale, you know what I mean?"

Just as Morgan was starting to pull on his jeans, the music stopped. Something was wrong; the whole room was ominously quiet. Morgan froze.

At the other end of the locker room, a Tuff's fist closed around a bunch of keys and tied them to one end of a wet towel in a nice solid knot. Another Tuff stuffed a fistful of quarters into the knotted bottom of another towel.

Morgan glanced up a moment before the weighted end of the wet towel hit the locker two inches behind his head. The locker cracked and dented. *Thwack!* The towel hit a bench. Morgan knew he was in for it. It was Eddie and Mickey with the towels, and Nick stood nearby, watching.

Morgan tried to edge away. "All right," he said gently, as though he were speaking to a rabid dog. "Okay."

He held his hands out. The towel slammed into his bare skin and Morgan bit his lip. Another towel hit, then another, vivid welts rising after each hit, and Morgan couldn't breathe for the pain. He couldn't fight them all. Still, he thought clearly through the panic, if I can just reach the locker-room door behind me, I can get out.

Eddie tripped him and he fell facedown onto a bench as the weighted towels rained across his back. Morgan closed his eyes and prayed.

Nick was the one who called them off, signaling to Mickey and Eddie, who stopped, frowning. They wanted to get it over with.

Hauser favored the more subtle approach. He

ran his finger across Morgan's swelling back. Morgan flinched. Hauser was calling it for what it was. Morgan knew he was powerless, a dead piece of meat.

"Ooh, nasty." Nick mocked him. "I don't know, man, I thought you were such a smart guy."

Morgan could barely breathe, but he refused to give in. He looked up at Nick.

Nick slammed his fist into Morgan's eye as a parting token of his goodwill. "That's for being stupid and messing around with my property."

Nick beckoned to the Tuffs and they split. Morgan was amazed at how cold the locker-room bench felt against his body. He lay there working it out. Maybe if he tried incredibly hard, he could drag himself off the bench and get over to Jimmy's place. Jimmy was his friend. Jimmy could help him out.

An hour and a half later, Morgan was sitting on a beat-up old couch in the Parkers' littered backyard as Jimmy swiped at his back with a bottle of disinfectant. Morgan was watching the Dobermans. He'd always heard Dobermans were sweet if you trained them right. Obviously, Donnie Parker trained them wrong. The Dobermans, command-trained to attack, barked incessantly as they paced in their wire cages.

"They ever stop barking?" Morgan asked.

"Nope. Trained. They sell faster that way."

"I don't see how you can stand it, man."

Jimmy grinned. "Why do you think I took up drumming? Aside from the fact that I'd rather have Donnie selling these wild beasts to the terrified middle classes instead of robbing liquor stores with Andy Hauser."

Morgan grunted, then winced. It didn't pay to move around too much.

"Sorry." Jimmy handed him some ice. "Here. Helps take the swelling down."

Morgan nodded just as Ronnie hurtled blindly breathless into the yard. "Jimmy, Jimmy," she called. "Nick found out about Frankie and he's ready to tear Morgan apart—"

"Thanks, Ron," Morgan and Jimmy deadpanned. "We heard."

Ronnie stopped, in shock. "Pain in my heart . . ."

David Hiller sat at the kitchen table, studying manuals that explained the intricacies of California real estate. Page came in with an armload of groceries.

"How's it coming?" she asked, looking as unruffled as ever. Elegantly overdressed for food shopping, she smiled at her husband.

"Okay. California real estate's really not so

different from Connecticut's. I should be ready to take the test in no time."

Page pulled out a loaf of bread. "Morgan home?"

"I haven't seen him—probably just got caught up with his friends."

The front door slammed.

"Morgan?" Page called, to no response.

The clock in the kitchen ticked loudly. Page started after her son, a tense pinched look replacing her smile. She wouldn't put up with any of Morgan's games, and she'd tell him so, though she doubted it would do any good.

"No," her husband said. "I'll go."

David Hiller walked over to his son's bedroom, knocked, then opened the door just as Morgan gingerly pulled off his shirt.

David took one look at his son's face and body. "What happened to you?"

Morgan didn't even try to smile. He was too sore to even shrug. "The same old thing that always happens. I screwed up." He shut his eyes. His ribs hurt; it felt like they were pressing right into his heart. He didn't want his father's sympathy. Not now. He hadn't been looking for trouble. Why was it trouble always found him so easily?

"Morgan." His father sounded calm and concerned. "I know this move has been hard on you, but if you're having problems, you have to come to me."

"And tell you what? The prodigal son's in trouble? Again?"

David was quiet for a minute. He knew the sarcasm merely masked the anguish underneath. He sat down on the bed, ready to hash this out calmly with his son. He wanted to understand Morgan, but the kid never gave him a chance.

"Just *cut* the self-righteous crap," David said. "So what if you make a mistake? Do you think I want you to end up like Brian? So afraid of failure you can't make a move without your mother's approval? No"—he shook his head—"that's just not you."

Morgan wished, for a moment, that he could talk to his father about things. After all, the man had known him for seventeen years already. Was he going to go through life failing everything he attempted without understanding why?

"What do I do right now?"

David looked at his wounded son and knew the question was a big concession. Memories flooded his mind. He remembered a much younger Morgan, always so serious and vulnerable. Morgan had always taken things too hard, too personally, and he'd hide behind a defensive wall. Yet underneath his tough exterior, David knew Morgan was a normal kid, struggling to live life his own way rather than the way Page or anyone else told him to live. David respected that in his son, and he wasn't going to wreck this chance to be close to him. After all, Morgan needed him.

"What you do is what you *know* is right," he said carefully. "What *you* believe in. Life is a mystery to be lived—so live it. Give yourself a break, Morgan. Take it easy on yourself."

Morgan felt love for his father surge through his aching muscles. Maybe someone actually did understand him. He wished he could tell his father thanks, but Page's footsteps echoed in the hallway. "David, Morgan—dinner's ready."

David got up and headed her off at the door. "Where's Morgan?" she asked just outside her son's room.

"Lying down," her husband told her.

"Is something wrong?"

David couldn't stand it when his wife jumped to conclusions.

"Nothing he can't handle."

Morgan grimaced as he struggled into a different shirt. "That's right," he mimicked. "Nothing I can't handle."

7

Several hours later across town, Frankie sat in front of the three-way dressing-table mirror her father had brought her from the Salvation Army. Three Frankie reflections frowned back at her.

The real Frankie took a deep breath and reached for the pile of articles she'd ripped out of the classy fashion magazines this afternoon. Ever since Friday night, Frankie had known she needed a make-over.

She picked through the articles, staring at page after page of fresh-faced models, their hair shiny, their complexions glowing, and their lips pouting sweetly. Frankie sucked in her cheeks and looked in the mirror again.

How did those dumb country-club girls know what to do? Maybe they were born that way, or maybe their mothers taught them. Frankie thought desperately of her mother and sighed. She picked up a jade-green eye-shadow pencil. No, too obvious.

Frankie glanced around her room at the clips she'd cut out of *Hit Parader* and plastered all over her walls. They looked stupid with her secondhand lace curtains. But she liked Mötley Crü and Johnny Rotten. Trouble was, she was changing. Nick didn't even know it, and Nick was her old boyfriend. Frankie shuddered ... Was she really thinking of Nick as her *old* boyfriend now?

She picked up a smoky-blue shadow. Now that was more like it.

When she heard her father's footsteps in the hall, Frankie grabbed a chair and shoved it under the doorknob. Frankie was wearing one of her mother's black lace camisoles over a matching black half-slip. It made her feel better, wearing something of her mother's, but she didn't want her father to know. Besides, she needed her privacy right now.

She looked at herself again. Then she looked at the clips on her wall.

"Yes, thank you," she mimicked overheard conversations from the country club. She picked up a lipstick brush. "I *am* fabulous. You?

Fabulous. No, I wouldn't care for any lobster tonight. I'm afraid we've been having it at home until it's running out my ears ... Yes, it *is* boring, but what's a girl to do?"

She looked woodenly at her new image, then threw the brush down in frustration. "Looks like I died."

She shook her head and hurried over to her rack of clothes, starting to plow through her wardrobe.

She pulled out a sexy tank top and held it up against her chest. Too trashy. She dumped it on the floor. Next. A bright-red off-the-shoulder job. Forget it.

Her father was calling from the hall. "Frankie, Nick's on his way over."

"Okay, thanks." Just what she needed right now. She wanted to be left alone.

Back to the clothes. A Day-Glo purple mini. No way. Why didn't she have any decent clothes? Frankie sorted through the hangers in desperation. She yanked out a white T with black suspender straps. That was it. She held it up under her neck and pivoted, like a model on a ramp, as she tried to decide if it was appropriate.

What the hell, she thought, and pulled it on. Next thing she knew, she thought she heard something like violins. And a *piano?* The melody was a tune with which she was not familiar, but she had a sneaking suspicion about who was making it happen. "No!" she said aloud, involuntarily. She stomped over to the window, yanked it up, and leaned out.

"Yes!" It echoed down the staircase. Yes.

Morgan was leaning against a wall in Frankie's backyard, his ghetto-blaster at his feet playing a cassette tape of Bach's Brandenburg Concerto #1 in F Major.

"Does that mean you like it?" he called up to her. Juliet on the balcony must have looked just like Frankie, he thought.

"No! I mean, I don't know . . ." Frankie was flustered. "Just turn it off so the neighbors don't start screaming."

"They don't care. They're too busy fighting to notice."

"My *father* isn't. So turn it off!"

Morgan turned it off, then moved painfully across the yard to the fire escape. "I thought you'd want to see me again."

"This isn't exactly what I had in mind," she said dryly.

Morgan took each step gingerly.

"What are you doing?" Frankie asked, horrified. She was beginning to realize that Morgan was real. This wasn't something she'd just dreamed up. What was worse, he was climbing up the fire escape to see her. This was no vision. Morgan wanted to see her as much as she wanted to see him—

"What does it look like, your room?"

"No! I mean, you can't—" He was nearly there.

"Why not? A room's a room."

"Yeah, but don't you remember some little incident in the locker room today?"

Morgan reached her window and gazed at her intently for just a second. Then he fell into her arms.

He makes me nuts, she thought. I'm out of control. Is this really happening? "Morgan, please"—she tried to pull out of his embrace—"I'm serious."

"So am I." So he was. Desperately serious about Frankie Croyden. Totally obsessed, possessed. If he didn't feel her respond—now, caught by surprise—then he would go crazy. He didn't want to know why this was happening. He didn't care. She was beautiful. Her hair smelled wonderful.

When Morgan kissed her, Frankie kissed him back without really understanding why. It made her angry.

She pulled back and tried to stay mad. "Great. Fine," she said. "So you kissed me. Now go away before Nick finds out you're here."

"I thought you liked taking risks."

"Yeah, when they're reasonable."

"What's so unreasonable about me?" He kissed her again, her lips, her cheeks, her ears, her hair.

More, Frankie breathed to herself. No one has ever kissed me like this before. "Nothing," she said aloud, then realized what she'd given away. Flustered, she added, "Everything. Now go away."

"Not till you explain."

"What's to explain?" Frankie was frustrated. Nick was going to show up any minute now. Didn't Morgan understand anything? Morgan was nothing but trouble. "I'm here. You're there. We don't fit."

"All I'm asking for is a shot."

"At what?" Frankie looked away from him to one of her *Wild Thing* posters. "It's not going to change anything."

Morgan was dead serious. "That chance is worth everything."

He bent to kiss her again.

Frankie heard a noise outside in the hall. Someone was walking toward her door and it wasn't her father. Frankie pulled away in panic as Nick began pounding on her door. "Frankie? Frankie! Open up. It's me!"

"Just a sec," she yelled, terrified, then whispered to Morgan. "*That's* why."

"Shall I get it?" Morgan asked blandly.

"No! What are you, crazy?"

Nick kept pounding on the door and rattling the doorknob.

"Frankie?" Morgan begged. "Would you come to dinner Friday night at my house? Please?"

"No."

"I wish you would, Frankie."

"I can't." I can—I will, Frankie thought. Why did he have to make her feel so confused? She couldn't think standing this close to him.

"Frankie?" Morgan was determined not to let her go until she said yes.

"*Frankie,*" Nick yelled, angry. "Open up already! What are you doing in there anyway?"

Frankie's eyes flashed from the door back to Morgan. "Okay, all right," she whispered. "Now get out of here."

As Morgan turned to go, he shoved a copy of Kerouac's *On the Road* in her hands. Bewildered, Frankie wondered why. But there was no time for questions. Morgan hurried over the window ledge, then leaned in to kiss her good-bye.

Frankie slammed the window shut, tossed the book on her bed, then quickly pulled the chair out from under the door.

Nick sauntered in, stuffing a Twinkie in his mouth. "What's your problem?"

Frankie couldn't even look at him. "No

problem," she replied. "Can't a girl have any privacy around here?"

"Sure," Nick said. "But not when me and your dad wanna celebrate."

"Celebrate?"

Mr. Croyden walked into Frankie's bedroom holding a bottle of good champagne and three glasses. Usually he looked tired and sad, but for the first time since her mother's death, Frankie saw him really smile. "That's right," he said. "It's not every night I get asked for my baby's hand."

Frankie started to shake. She hated Nick. It just couldn't be true. "*What?*"

"Yep," Nick said, "and he said yes, too. What's the matter? You know, for a girl who's about to get married, you don't look all that happy." Nick took the bottle from Mr. Croyden and turned it over. "How do you open this thing, anyway?"

Frankie's father gave her a hug. "I'm so happy, sweetheart. I only wish Mama was here to share it."

Frankie buried her head in her father's shoulder, then sneaked a peek at Nick. Her fiancé. If only Morgan . . . she couldn't think about it.

Nick was smirking and Frankie knew he was thinking it was too late for the bebop. She was his. Her father had said so. What was she supposed to do anyway? She knew as well as anybody that it was a jungle out there and that she needed protection from people like Morgan Hiller. If Nick's kind of protection was all she could get, that's what she had to live with, there wasn't really any choice. But if there wasn't any choice, then why had she agreed to go to Morgan's place for dinner? Maybe she was changing more than she thought.

The cork exploded with a huge pop and Frankie's heart broke. She closed her eyes and hugged her father more tightly than ever, wishing his embrace could protect her, wishing she could stay a little girl forever.

As he was leaving school the next day, all Morgan could think about was Frankie coming to dinner on Friday. Frankie sitting at the dining-room table, her hair all soft around her face . . .

"Hey! Wait up!"

Morgan turned to see Jimmy following him across campus, wheeling an ancient one-speed that looked like it'd been resurrected from the city dump.

"So what do you think?" Jimmy asked, awfully pleased with himself.

"It's great, man." An image flashed in Morgan's head of Nick and Frankie on his ten-speed, circling, taunting him. *Frankie* . . .

"Hey, I want you to have it. You know . . . consolation prize," Jimmy said.

"Consolation for what? I feel fine."

"Maybe you're right," Jimmy went on. "She can still change her mind. I mean, they probably won't get married till after graduation anyway."

Morgan started to get a sick feeling in his stomach, like he'd been punched.

"What?"

Oh, God, Jimmy thought, he didn't know. And Jimmy had foot-in-mouth disease. "Nick asked Frankie to marry him. Didn't—"

Morgan grabbed Jimmy's bike, leapt on it, and pedaled away.

"Where are you going?" Jimmy shouted.

"To find out her answer," Morgan yelled over his shoulder.

"Oh, man," Jimmy said, "it isn't worth it. Why can't you give it up?"

Morgan's mind was a frozen blank, a wasteland. She can't . . . she can't . . . she can't, he told himself as he pedaled furiously. The voice of the crusty old security guard barely made a dent in his consciousness.

"You!" The old guy was screaming. "You can't take that bike on campus!"

Morgan pedaled on.

"You can't ride on it, either!"

She can't . . . she can't . . . she can't.

*   *   *

Feather and Ronnie spent a lot of time with Frankie that day. News travels fast. Frankie didn't look all that happy; she was standing in the hall, jamming her books into her locker. Ronnie, however, was in a great mood. She was wearing one of Jimmy's shirts, the one with the palm trees on it.

"So are you going to get a ring?" Feather asked. Today her scarf was deep blue.

Frankie shrugged.

"Well, if you do," Ronnie said, "you should go on over to Woolworth's. Susan Ristelli got hers there and it almost looks like the real thing . . ."

Frankie slammed the locker door shut. The last thing she needed right now was to hear these two going on about how exciting it was to get married to Nick.

"Hot damn!" Ronnie screamed, throwing her hands up to her face and jumping up and down. "Will you just take a look at that?"

Frankie turned around to see Morgan ride up on an ancient old bike that he'd pedaled right down the middle of the high-school hall. He grabbed her arm. "I have to talk to you."

He didn't even give her a chance to open her mouth; he hoisted her right up onto the handlebars and pedaled away down the corridor.

"Wow!" Ronnie stared after them in amazement and admiration. "Total romance!" How did she do it?

The bike careened down the hall, popped a small wheelie going out the high-school doors, and skidded to a stop outside the south classroom building. Frankie hopped off and tried to act like a normal person.

"I thought you were coming to dinner Friday night."

"Well, I am!" Frankie screamed. "Who do you think you are, anyway?"

"When? After the wedding?"

"Look, don't start, okay? I have no control over that."

"Really. No control over your own life?"

"What do you know?"

"Maybe more than you think. Why don't you try me?"

"Why don't you drop dead and leave me alone? You're completely destroying my whole life. Everything was great until you came along."

"You call decoying for Nick a great life? Well, I'm sorry, but I don't happen to share your opinion. You're better than that."

"Just like those girls at the country club, right?"

"What are you, kidding me? You got it all wrong, Frankie. You want to walk around in a Shetland sweater for the rest of your life? Bet you don't even know they itch like hell. Don't you understand? All those guys were staring at you because they thought you were *beautiful.* And you are, I can't . . . you can't . . ."

"Go for it!" someone called out.

Frankie and Morgan looked around. They were in the middle of a bunch of kids and all the kids were watching them.

Frankie couldn't stand it anymore. She turned to walk away, but Morgan couldn't let her go without a firm answer. "Well?" he asked. "Are you still coming on Friday night?"

Frankie paused, then nodded. Yes.

Yes, she would come.

Across the campus another person had stopped to watch. He blinked. It couldn't be . . .

Nick Hauser felt the blood in his veins turn to ice and his heart freeze. Then the rage began and something inside of him snapped. A pure sweet image of Frankie danced for a moment in front of him, and then deliberately, Nick shot it down in flames forever.

8

Friday night Morgan paced restlessly around the living room until the doorbell rang. "I'll get it," he called, making a dash for the door.

Page and David exchanged glances. "Go easy tonight," David said. "This means a lot to him."

Page tried not to snap back, but she did anyway. "So did that girl he brought home for Easter last year. Remember? She was so stoned all she could do was stare at her peas and say, 'Wow, they're so green!' "

"That was different. He's trying now."

"So am I."

Frankie was practically catatonic she was so nervous. She wiped her hands down the sides of her bright-blue mini-dress. She couldn't do anything about the color of her dress, but she'd substituted her mother's single strand of pearls for the chain necklaces she usually wore. Frankie had also toned down her makeup, but that wasn't the only reason her face looked softer. Frankie was in love, and she was breathtakingly beautiful.

Morgan opened the door and stared at Frankie. She looked so vulnerable and lovely that all his fears dissolved. She had to be his.

"You look terrific," he said.

They stared at each other. Then Frankie took a deep breath and pulled out Morgan's battered copy of *On the Road*. "I brought your book," she said, walking through the door. "It was good. A little sad, but good. I mean, I've never met anybody who felt about things that way."

"Yeah," Morgan said. He couldn't take his eyes off her. He gave her a kiss on the forehead for luck. And hoped his mother would keep her mouth shut.

Neither of them saw the rust-colored Camaro parked down the street. Nick and Mickey and Eddie, sitting inside on the front seat, watched Frankie go inside the house. Nick's fingers were clenched so tightly on the steering wheel that his knuckles ached. The rage in him was white-hot. His head was on fire.

That's it, bebop, he repeated to himself. Over and over. That's it, bebop. Bebop. Bebop. Bebop.

She can't.

Without warning he opened his door, and got out, and walked up to the Hillers' house, a worried Eddie trailing behind him. He crouched under the dining-room window, where he could watch everything.

The girl sitting at the Hiller dining-room table wasn't Frankie. She looked like Frankie, but she sure wasn't the Frankie he knew. The other Frankie had made him feel good. This one made him furious every time he saw her.

Morgan wondered if his mother had chosen fettuccine deliberately because it was hard to manage. He squirmed in his chair and looked at Page Hiller, chattering away, oblivious to Frankie's discomfort. Morgan smiled at Frankie in reassurance.

Page yammered on. "You would have loved spending time with us in Connecticut, Frankie . . . skiing in the winter, boating in the summer. It was absolutely wonderful." She effortlessly twisted a forkful of noodles and raised it to her mouth. "Morgan was really quite a good yachtsman, too. Much better than Brian, in his own way." She gave Morgan the half-second once-over. "If he would have put some heart into it, there's no telling what he could have done."

David looked at his wife, wishing she'd stop talking for two minutes.

"Of course, none of that matters now." She forced a nonchalant tone. "I mean, since we moved."

Morgan dropped his fork loudly on his plate.

Outside, Nick couldn't stand to watch anymore. He turned around and pushed Eddie out of the way. "Get the hell out of here," he said in a furious whisper.

Eddie shrugged and went back to the car. Girls were always trouble. He got in the backseat and started yawning.

"Hiller," Nick said under his breath, not budging for the moment, "I'm gonna take your world apart one piece at a time."

David cleared his throat. He'd had enough. Frankie seemed terribly uncomfortable and he knew it was up to him to put her at ease. "Have you lived here all your life, Frankie?" he asked, trying to steer the conversation toward what was familiar to her.

"Yeah," she replied. "I mean . . . yes. All my life." She smiled apprehensively.

Morgan smiled too. God, she was beautiful.

Unfortunately, Page jumped in once again. "Then you must tell us all about the Huntington Gardens. I hear they are absolutely *fabulous*."

Morgan and Frankie smothered laughter as they thought of Ronnie at another dinner.

"Frankie doesn't really go for things like that, Mom. She spends most of her spare time reading."

Page didn't think Frankie was the reading type. Still, she forced a smile. "If you've never been to Huntington Gardens, maybe we should go. You can bring your mother and we'll make a day of it."

Morgan instantly knew his mother had said the worst. Frankie tried hard not to burst into tears, but there was a lump in her throat. She reached for her drink, but her hands were shaking so much she knocked over the glass, spilling soda all over the front of her blue mini-dress. She jumped up in alarm.

Page quickly took control. "It's all right. These things happen. Quick, Frankie, run and put cold water on your dress before it stains."

David stood up, ready to help, but Frankie hurried into the kitchen, mortified. She couldn't believe how nervous these people made her.

Morgan was furious with his mother and her infernal attitudes. She'd done it again. "Goddamnit, Mom, her mother's dead."

"Well, how was I supposed to know that?"

"Morgan, go help Frankie," his father said calmly.

"I don't know," Page protested. "It was an honest mistake, for God's sake . . ."

Morgan glared at his mother, infuriated by her insensitivity, and hurried into the kitchen. Frankie had soaked the entire front of her dress.

"Ruined," she said. "Everything is ruined."

"Here, let me help," Morgan offered, wanting to take her into his arms and tell her that he loved her, that his parents didn't matter, that she was all that he cared about.

Frankie turned away from him. She couldn't bear his seeing her humiliation. "I can *manage*, thank you." She tried to wipe the tears off her face. "Why don't you just go out there and talk about *roses* or something."

"She didn't mean anything by the Gardens." Morgan couldn't believe he was defending his mother.

"Great," Frankie said. She couldn't fight the tears any longer. "How can you stand it?"

Her question surprised him and he responded without even thinking. "It's my *family*."

That was it. Total humiliation. "I'm *going*." She stormed out of the kitchen, stalked through the dining room, and yanked the front door open.

"Frankie?" Page called. She looked at Morgan as he hurried after Frankie. "Is she leaving?"

"What do you think?" he yelled at her.

Frankie was halfway across the Hillers' lawn before Morgan caught up with her and grabbed her arm. "Come on, Frankie, we have to talk."

Frankie yanked her arm away. "Excuse me, I promised Ronnie I'd meet her at Woolworth's to look at wedding rings."

"Frankie, you don't belong with Nick."

"Maybe not, but I sure as hell don't belong with you." She ran off down the block, tears blinding her steps.

Morgan started after her, but his father had come outside and now he held him back. "Let her go. She feels humiliated."

Morgan faced his father, anger and hurt and bitterness in his eyes. He'd fucked up again. "No shit." He quickly walked off in the opposite direction.

He didn't see the rust-colored Camaro parked under a tree. Or the three pairs of eyes watching. Two were filled with anger. But one was filled with something far more chilling.

Mickey and Eddie trailed Morgan's progress down the street.

"You wanna take him out now?" Mickey asked.

Nick shook his head. He started the car. "I gotta go find my girlfriend."

9

Frankie turned the corner and marched down the sidewalk. She really didn't know where she was, and she didn't care. She just had to move.

She looked down at the red patch on her blue dress. Total ruin. And Morgan had wanted to help her, she thought, when he came into the kitchen. She hadn't let him. She didn't fit in Morgan's life. At least Nick didn't make her confused or expect her to be something she wasn't.

The rust-colored Camaro crept down the street behind her, and Nick pulled up slowly before poking his head out the window, his face a mask of innocence and surprise.

"Hey, baby," Nick said. "I've been looking all over for you."

Frankie shook her head and wiped the tears off her cheeks. She kept walking. The car trailed her slowly.

"Frankie?"

She paused. Nick wanted her for who she was. Slowly, she walked over to the car, opened the door, and got in. Nick put his arm around her and pulled her closer to him, grinning over the top of her head at Mickey and Eddie.

Frankie couldn't stop crying. "I'm sorry," she said, trying not to hiccup. "I'm just so confused."

"I know. Shhh." He kissed her gently, held her as if she were a child who'd skinned her knee. He glanced at Eddie. "Hey, man, hand me that bottle . . . thanks. Here, baby, here." He forced Frankie to take a sip. "Guaranteed to clear things up in a shot. Better?"

Frankie nodded.

Mickey and Eddie looked at each other. Had Nick finally lost it or what?

"That's my girl. Give me a kiss."

Frankie smiled shyly.

"Come on, please. Just one." Oh, Frankie. He brushed a kiss on her hair. Same hair, but this wasn't his Frankie. This was Frankie the imposter. His Frankie would never set foot in Morgan Hiller's house. The rage started up again, spidering up through his veins, white-hot.

His eyes narrowed as he looked in the rear-view mirror. "So whaddaya think? Feel like kickin' up a little dust?"

"Yeah."

"Great."

Mickey and Eddie leaned back, relieved. Nick was back to normal.

Many minutes later the Camaro cruised slowly down Van Nuys Boulevard, Frankie dozing in the front seat while Mickey and Eddie fidgeted in the backseat.

"Hey, man, how much longer?" Mickey complained. "We've been drivin for hours."

"And we'll keep driving till I find what I'm looking for," Nick said.

"Well, I sure hope we find it soon. I'm about to pee my pants," Mickey said drunkenly.

"So shove it out the window, stupid," Eddie said, equally drunk. "Use your head."

They were all hopeless, Nick thought as he kept driving.

David Hiller got out of his yellow checker cab for a stretch. He exchanged greetings with another cabbie and bought a newspaper from the box on the street. Another al-fresco breakfast at dawn. He stifled a yawn. He was getting tired of this routine.

Nick turned the corner and saw the cab. That

was Morgan's father standing right there, oblivious to anything but the real-estate section.

Nick jammed on the brakes and the car jerked to a stop, waking Frankie up.

"Shit, I don't believe it. We're running out of gas."

Frankie sat up and rubbed her eyes. "What?" she asked sleepily.

"I *said*"—Nick felt the rage surging in him— "we're running out of gas." He pulled off his watch. "Here, take this. Go ask that cabbie if he'll trade it for some cash."

Frankie was irritated out of her sleepiness. "But I gave you that watch, Nick. Don't you have any money?"

"Do you think I'd trade it if I did? Now, move."

Frankie made a face, yanked the car door open, and started across the street. Then she saw the cabbie.

She stopped, surprised. And then she realized, as every nerve in her body started jangling like a fire alarm, why she was here and what Nick was after.

Frankie quickly turned around and went back to the Camaro. She couldn't—she just—

"I can't do it, Nick. I'd rather walk than trade that watch." Frankie tried to sound nonchalant.

"Why?"

Frankie thought she would scream.

"Because it's Hiller's father?" Nick asked, glaring at her. The other Frankie. He smacked his hand across her face. "I asked you a question!"

"Yes!" Frankie screamed.

"You shoulda thought of that before you got involved. Now move it!"

"No!"

"I said move!"

Frankie moved. She started slowly across the street, then broke into a run, terrified, her hair swinging wildly. "Mr. Hiller," she yelled, "go!"

"Frankie?" David looked up from the morning edition. "What's going on? Are you in trouble?"

"Please," Frankie was sobbing, "just go—"

When Mickey and Eddie rushed David from behind, Frankie tried her best to pull them off, but Mickey grabbed her hard and threw her to the ground.

David kneed Eddie and then laid one squarely in Mickey's gut. But there were two of them and they were young and out for blood. He wasn't a match for them.

"Run, Frankie," he yelled, "run!"

Frankie tried to pull herself up as David tried to break away to help her.

She looked up and saw Nick reach under his sweatshirt.

That's when she saw the gun. It was black, and long, and the muzzle was a gaping wide hole that had death written all over it. Frankie froze, but Nick wasn't looking at her.

Nick was looking at David, and as rage filled his eyes, his finger pulled the trigger. The gun sounded like a bomb exploding.

A moment later, a red stain spread across David's chest and David fell in a heap on the sidewalk.

Mickey and Eddie stared in stupefied shock, then realized where they were and what Nick had done. Nick turned and ran.

Call the police, Frankie's mind screamed. Get help. Do something. She tried to force her numb legs to move. Get up! But she couldn't get up and she beat the sidewalk with her fist in frustration.

"No," she sobbed. "*No—*"

10

Morgan walked the hospital corridors until he came to his father's room. He walked through the door, over to David's bed.

"Dad? Dad, it's Morgan. Can you hear me?"

No response. David Hiller was on the critical list, tubes connecting his body to the intensive-care equipment, his link to life. The steady ping of the cardiac monitor filled Morgan's ears.

"Dad?"

A nurse put her hand gently on Morgan's shoulder. "I'm sorry, but the doctor says he shouldn't exert himself."

Morgan nodded and went to find his mother. Page was sitting in the waiting room, staring at the cracks in the green linoleum tiles. She didn't see her son come in.

She looks helpless, Morgan thought when he sat down. She seemed tortured. Is that how I make her feel? Morgan asked himself. He felt guilt wash through him and he wanted to reach out and hug her, but his arms faltered. What was he so afraid of?

"Mom?" He touched her shoulder and she turned to him, anguished. For just one second, they connected. Instantly, Morgan knew he and his mother understood each other for the first time in years. They both loved the man who was critically hurt in the next room, and that shared emotion brought them together.

Then Morgan saw Brian walking down the hall. Page actually smiled and ran into the out-stretched arms of her son. "Oh, Brian," she sobbed.

He held her tight. "Shh, Mom, it's okay, it'll be okay. I'm here. Don't worry."

He didn't even look in his brother's direction, but at that moment Morgan noticed someone else walking down the hall. Frankie. Disheveled, bloody, and shaking. She stood like a zombie, preparing herself for the worst.

Morgan ran to her, and she threw her arms around him, desperate for his touch, for the fact that he was real and she wasn't going to die and the picture of that long black tunnel at the end of the gun would go away and he would just hold her and she'd be okay.

He engulfed her in his embrace. She was his.

"I'm sorry," she managed to stutter. "I'm so sorry . . ."

Frankie felt her legs sag in relief.

"Shh. It's all right. The doctors say he'll be all right." Morgan brushed the hair off her forehead, noticing the bruises on her face.

Suddenly something clicked inside Morgan's head. He shut his eyes. *How had she known?*

Cold, sickening anger filled his chest. Nick. Nick Hauser shot his father. Morgan looked at Frankie, who was sobbing quietly in his arms. Nick could've killed her too. He was probably sorry he hadn't, the way things had turned out.

Frankie hiccuped and nestled deeper into his arms. Frankie needed him and his father would be okay. But Nick Hauser had shot his father.

"Come on, Frankie," Morgan whispered. "Let's go home." He walked her out to the parking lot, got her into his parents' car, and drove her to his house. But it wasn't until he got her into his room and sat her on his bed that she started to act anything like the Frankie he knew.

"Ouch!" Frankie grimaced, flinching as Morgan wiped one of her cuts with Betadine. She sat at the foot of his bed, wearing one of his button-down oxford-cloth shirts. Morgan had never seen her look so beautiful.

"Sorry, it's a bad one."

Frankie tried to smile. "I know, I can feel it clear into next week."

"You want me to stop?"

She shook her head. A tear trickled down her cheek and she sniffed. "I'm sorry. I just keep hearing that gun go off over and over again." She stared at him. "It's like a razor slicing my heart, you know?"

"Yeah, I know."

Frankie searched his eyes. "How do you deal with it?"

"I don't." He kissed away a tear. "I just keep exploding."

"I thought things were supposed to be easy when you had money."

Morgan unbuttoned the top button of her shirt. "Only when you don't take it seriously."

"But how do you do that?"

He unbuttoned another. "By letting it go." He smiled, a flash of the old sardonic Morgan. "The only way to hold on to something is to let it go."

He kissed her, gently at first. And then again and again. He waited to make this one moment last forever. Nothing else existed except the feel of Frankie in his arms.

Frankie thought she must be dreaming, but this wasn't the nightmare the last few hours had been. This was heaven. She was safe. She was loved.

She reached to caress Morgan's cheek. He *was* real, after all. She started to unbutton his shirt and they smiled shyly at each other.

This was what Morgan had meant a long time ago in a different world. There was more. Much, much more. And Frankie had never been happier.

Morgan rode Frankie home on the handlebars of Jimmy's decrepit one-speed. She didn't want to go, but her father would be worrying— and Morgan's father was worrying his son.

Frankie hopped off the bike in front of Croyden Liquors and flung her arms around Morgan to kiss him good-bye. They laughed. They kissed again, then Frankie ran into the store.

Morgan pedaled on, happily oblivious of the fact that the rust-colored Camaro was parked down the street from Croyden Liquors.

Nick didn't know how long he had been sitting there staring at Frankie's father's store, but he'd been there long enough to remember everything. Frankie's room. The posters on the wall. *Wild Thing.* Her bed. Her hair spread all around her. Her smile. Her skinny little butt that fit perfectly on the handlebars of a bike. *Morgan's* bike. The scene in the parking lot came back in stunning clarity. The intense revving of the engine. In his mind, the Camaro roared into action once more and the bike crashed to the ground.

Nick opened the car door.

Frankie sat perched on the counter, a makeshift confessional, and told her father everything.

"Of course I just want you to be happy. I just thought that you and Nick—"

"—had a good thing goin', huh, baby?" Nick finished the sentence for him.

Frankie looked at him, terrified. "Nick—"

For just half a second he thought he saw the old Frankie, but now she was really and truly gone. This was the new Frankie, the one who'd betrayed him.

"I saw you, bitch," he screamed as he grabbed her on the counter and slapped her across the room. Mr. Croyden, furious, moved behind Nick to stop him, but Nick couldn't be stopped. He shoved Frankie's father away into a display of liquor bottles and cartons.

Frankie snapped. How dare he? How dare he touch her father?

She leapt on him, piggyback, and dug into his face with her nails. "You bastard! You don't own me!"

He threw her off. "I do own you. And I'll do what I goddamn want with you, bitch."

Frankie tried to get up but Nick backhanded her down again.

"No—please—don't."

"It's too late now, baby. You shoulda ..
Shit." He cursed violently. For a minute the
rage in his head cleared. What was he doing?

Mr. Croyden moaned as he tried to get up
and Frankie looked at her bleeding hands. But
it wasn't his Frankie—it was the other one.

Nick yanked Frankie, by the hair, to her feet
and hauled her over to the telephone.

"C'mon, let's call your *new* boyfriend. I wanna
have a word with him."

Morgan was in the kitchen when the phone
rang.

Frankie's voice was hysterical.

"Morgan, stay away! He'll kill you—he'll—"

Nick snatched the receiver.

"Listen good, bebop. Nobody takes anything
from me, understand. I'll kill it before I give it
up." He paused, thinking. "If you wanna watch,
be at the Warehouse in twenty minutes."

Click. Dial tone.

Morgan stared at the phone, his pulse racing.
Stay calm, he told himself, and plan your moves.

Brian walked into the kitchen. Impeccable
timing, as usual. "I want to talk to you," he
announced, thinking he would soon have everything under control.

"Okay," Morgan said as he headed for his

room. "You can start by telling me how Dad is."

Brian followed him. "A little better . . . asking for you. Now, why don't you tell me what kind of trouble you're in before the police get here?"

"It's nothing I can't handle." Morgan rummaged in his dresser drawer for his dart guns. Where were those darts? The professional ones. Steel-tipped.

"Don't get smart with me, Morgan."

Just who the hell did Golden Boy think he was now? Morgan had swallowed his attitude all his life, and wasn't about to choke down any more.

"Or you'll *what?*" Morgan said coldly but calmly. "Tell me what a waste I am? Give me a lecture on the rules of the game?" He found the darts and placed them in his pocket. Jimmy's knife was in there too, a comforting omen. "Well, I hate to tell you, big brother, but the rules have changed. Your rules have never have been mine. They'll never be mine. Just like mine will never be yours. Why is that so hard for you to comprehend? Didn't they teach you anything in any of those fancy schools?" He headed for the door.

Brian put his arm up to block the way. Morgan stared him down.

Nothing the Golden Boy could say or do would hurt him anymore. Not now. Not ever.

Brian blanched at the look in Morgan's eyes, and he moved his arm out of the way. "If you leave this house, I'll have you picked up within twenty-four hours."

Morgan hurried out. "Great. I can use all the help I can get tonight."

Brian stared at his retreating back.

Over at the Parkers', Donnie was engrossed in a car chase on TV, teasing one of his babies, the Doberman named Daisy, with a Cheese Doodle. Donnie took a slug of beer.

Morgan knocked before he opened the door. The dogs barked in response. Donnie silenced them with a command.

"Is Jimmy here?"

"No." Donnie didn't bother to look at him.

"Do you know where he is?"

Donnie shook his head, picked up the remote control, and changed stations. Stupid faggots in their cars.

Morgan hastily scribbled a note. "If you see him, give him this. Okay?" He put the note in the middle of the coffee table, on top of the empty beer cans and a crumpled Doritos bag.

Donnie finally looked at Morgan and immediately knew something was wrong. Even the dogs could feel it. They growled in the back of their throats. Bad vibes.

"What is it, your will?"

The door slammed.

11

Nick was on stage at the Warehouse. Director and star. This was his command performance and he was calling all the shots.

Frankie, for instance, was standing, in a daze, on the cold cement blocks that served as the Warehouse's stage. Mascara made dark tracks of her tears. She looked like her eyes had melted.

Pathetic, Nick thought. The other Frankie wouldn't stand there helplessly, crying to herself.

The Tuffs milled around nervously.

Nick saw the sentry appear at the top of the wraparound balcony. "Hey!" Nick called to him. "Move back to where I told you." Stupid fool.

Mickey finished spray-painting the Tuff logo downstairs. They'd been waiting for hours, it seemed. Eddie was bored out of his brain, and he looked at another Tuff, then shook his head.

"Hey, Nick," Mickey finally asked, "how much longer do we hafta wait?"

"Till we *have* to."

"How can you do this?" Frankie asked.

Nick stared at her. Pathetic. "How can you do this?" he mimicked. "You don't even care," he spat at her. She looked like a little lost dog. Dumb bitch. "C'mon, puppy. Get down on your knees. Little puppy dog."

Slowly, Frankie sank to her knees. Morgan, she implored silently, don't come. I don't care anymore, but Nick's gonna kill you. I saw the look in his eyes. Stay away—

But Morgan Hiller didn't stay away. He came prepared.

The bored sentry heard a noise and whirled around, his broken-off antenna ready to hand. It was the same one that had slashed the Japanese patch on Morgan's leather jacket.

An eye for an eye, a tooth for a tooth, Morgan thought. A slash for a slash.

The two faced each other, crouching. The sentry was too absorbed to even think of calling for assistance. He was a Tuff, after all.

Morgan pulled out his dart gun and the sentry stopped cold, then started to panic.

That one second hesitation was all Morgan needed to pistol-whip the bastard and watch the kid fall in a silent heap, out cold.

Tuff luck, chump, Morgan said to himself as he looked around, plotting his next move. He peered out over one of the billboards and saw Nick and Frankie, Mickey and Eddie, and the other Tuff near the staircase . . . what luck.

There were ropes tied loosely over the railings, support for the giant tacky billboards hanging around the Warehouse. Ringling Brothers Circus. "Enjoy!"

Morgan grabbed one of the ropes, loosened it, knotted an end over the balcony, and tied the other end to the unconscious sentry's feet. Then he went back to the railing to loosen the rest of the ropes.

Meanwhile, Nick grabbed Frankie's hair and pulled hard. "Look at me!" he screamed. "I don't know who you are anymore." Why was he still going to fight for her?

Nick heard a whistle, a melody. It couldn't be.

"Bebop a lu la . . ."

Frankie heard it. "Oh, baby, no," she said softly.

Mickey and Eddie looked up too.

"Bebop a lu la . . ."

Morgan let the ropes fly and the billboard

came crashing down on Mickey's and Eddie's heads, knocking them out cold. The hapless sentry flew in the air, hanging upside down.

Carrying a length of rusty pipe as a weapon, the remaining Tuff charged up the stairs, but Morgan was waiting for him.

He drew his dart gun and fired. Darts hit the guy in the hands and he screamed in pain. Morgan kicked him down the stairs and he fell in a heap at the bottom. This was war.

Nick aimed the gun and fired. A bullet splintered the railing, inches from Morgan. Nick fired again and this time Morgan lurched back.

"Okay, Hiller," Nick yelled, "the fun's over. Get your ass down here or I blow her brains out!" He paused. "Hiller," he screamed.

Morgan crept up the stairs, then ran around the balcony, aiming for a long hanging rope that could get him down to the stage.

Nick heard him run across the balcony, pointed the gun, and pulled the trigger. A bullet splintered the railing.

Frankie couldn't stand it one more second. She jumped Nick, grabbing for the gun to deflect the next shot. When Nick tried to slap her down, she bit his hand and he dropped the gun. Nick hit her and this time she fell.

Morgan grabbed the rope and swung, like Errol Flynn in *The Adventures of Robin Hood*, down from the balcony. His momentum knocked

Nick down, feetfirst onto the stage. The gun spun away out of reach. Morgan and Nick were on each other like two wild animals. But Morgan's fury weighted his fists, and finally he had Hauser where he wanted him: he was paying him back for every week of torture, for everything—

Morgan raised his fist and time stopped. For an instant, he looked into Nick's fearful, hate-filled eyes and saw a mirror reflection of himself.

Morgan didn't hear them coming, because he'd forgotten all about Mickey and Eddie until they grabbed his arms.

Nick shook his head to clear it, then got up slowly. He searched for the gun and found it, picked it up, and jiggled its weight in his hand. He cocked the trigger. "So, bebop, how's the silver spoon feel now? Huh?"

Morgan stared death in the face. This was it.

"Huh, asshole?"

The gun was about to go off when a door slammed in the deserted Warehouse. It was Jimmy, with two of Donnie's Dobermans. The dogs were straining at their leashes, growling as Jimmy seized up the situation instantly.

"Aus!" he said, releasing the dogs. They took off. And Mickey and Eddie took off . . . in opposite directions.

Nick crouched and fired. The shot missed the dogs but hit Jimmy in the leg. Jimmy looked down, stupefied, clutched his leg, and slid to the floor, semiconscious.

The dogs continued the chase. Eddie crashed through a window followed by a Doberman. Mickey climbed up a pole. The other dog, barking furiously, kept him treed, shaking for his life.

Morgan slammed into Nick, knocking the gun from his hands. "You bastard. You shot Jimmy. You shot my father. I'll kill you."

They fought each other wildly until Nick knocked Morgan hard in the gut and Morgan fell, winded, gasping for breath. Nick fell on top of him.

Frankie stood over them both with the gun in her hands. She was perfectly calm. She pointed the gun at Nick. "Let him go, Nick."

Nick let Morgan fall. Frankie, gun in hand, loomed over him, her face set.

"Frankie—"

"Are there any bullets left, Nick? Maybe one for my father too? Or Morgan? How many are left?" Her hands weren't even trembling.

Nick tried to smile nervously, but he couldn't. This was the old Frankie. The Tuff one.

"Hey, baby," he implored, "I did it for you—"

"You didn't do it for me," Frankie spat back. "You did it for yourself."

Nick reached for her.

"Now move back," she yelled.

Nick stepped toward her and Frankie pulled the trigger. The gun clicked on an empty chamber. Frankie's eyes widened in horror when she realized what she'd done. She hadn't meant to, but she *had* pulled the trigger.

Nick couldn't believe it. Frankie had pulled the trigger. She had actually tried to shoot him.

Morgan saw Nick hit Frankie and he watched as the gun flew out of her hand and she fell off the stage onto the dance floor. Morgan got up and ran over to where Frankie lay, motionless. He looked at Nick in rage and fury. The first thing he could find to grab was an ax, and Morgan picked it up and began swinging.

Eyes wide with fear, Nick ran up the stairs and tripped. In the distance they heard the far echo of police sirens, but Morgan kept swinging, Nick scrambling for his life. Morgan chased Nick up the stairs until the ax flew out of his hands and he and Nick were fighting one on one as equals, as partners, as fools, both for the same thing, but for no reason at all. They pounded at each other until Nick was slumped on the balcony. Morgan turned to run down the stairs to Frankie.

But Hauser wasn't down yet. He pulled himself up by the balcony railing, grabbed a two-by-four, and started swinging, but he fell over the rail and landed on the floor below.

Morgan felt no remorse, no rage, nothing.

The fight had gone out of him. He looked down on the unconscious Nick. "I'm *real* sorry, Hauser," he mumbled as he groped his way down the stairs, "but you wouldn't have it any other way."

As Morgan reached the bottom of the stairs, Frankie staggered into his arms. He held her tight. She was alive, they were both okay. Morgan listened as the sirens grew closer and stopped. A door slammed; two cops ran in and one of them asked, "What's the story here?"

"My friend needs help," Morgan shouted. "He's been shot."

"And the other one?" The cop motioned toward Nick.

"Yeah, he needs help too." Morgan and Frankie hurried over to Jimmy, who lay in a pool of blood. Jimmy barely managed a smile. One of the Dobermans trotted over, Mickey's knife in its mouth.

EPILOGUE

The doorman at Club 60s remembered Frankie. He let her and her boyfriend in for free again. And he let her add two names to the guest list.

Jack Mack was on stage again too. He remembered Frankie. Same crazy long hair, same crazy smile; only now she looked different, softer, like a flower in bloom.

Morgan looked happier too, he and Frankie were dancing close. Young love, and not a care in the world.

Jimmy, in a walking cast nearly up to his hip, hobbled in looking for someone. He saw his friends and waved. Frankie and Morgan rushed over to Jimmy and gave him a hug as the go-go dancers shimmied in approval.

"Whoa, check it out," Jimmy said, pointing to his graffiti-embellished cast. "State of the arts."

Ronnie sauntered in. She had lots of tiny ribbons tied in her hair and she was lookin' good. Two guys went up to her right away and one of them asked her to dance, but she shook her head. She was looking for somebody. She saw Jimmy and smiled. State of the arts.

Jack Mack launched into another tune: "You're the reason all the boys come back for more . . ."

He sang to Frankie as the horn players leapt off the stage and hit the dance floor. It seemed as if everyone was playing for Frankie tonight. Jimmy could get into it.

He grabbed a trumpet and started to play as the crowd laughed. Someone handed Morgan a sax and he tried his best. Frankie and Ronnie joined in as the band on stage kept up the backbeat while the colored lights flashed and the dancers moved in rhythm.

In short, it was just another one of those enchanted evenings.

Great Reading from SIGNET VISTA

Stories of Courage from SIGNET and SIGNET VISTA

(0451)

☐ **CHERNOWITZ! by Fran Arrick.** Bobby could handle a bully—but anti-Semitism was something else.... "A frightening reminder that the spread of racial prejudice can happen anywhere."—*Horn Book*
(122860—$2.25)

☐ **KIM'S WINTER by Molly Wyatt.** When her parents die, sophisticated seventeen-year-old Kim Carpenter must adjust to a very different kind of life in a small New England town. (114353—$1.75)*

☐ **A BOAT TO NOWHERE by Maureen Crane Wartski.** The story of three Vietnamese children and their grandfather who leave the dangers of their village to become boat people searching for freedom in another country. "... the tragedy of the Vietnamese people, and the triumph of their spirit over intense adversity, is beautifully told ..."—Alton Kastner, deputy director, International Rescue Committee
(096789—$1.50)

☐ **A LONG WAY FROM HOME by Maureen Crane Wartski.** A sequel to *A Boat To Nowhere*, this is the story of the sometimes painful, yet ultimately successful adjustment to life in America for three Vietnamese children. (114345—$1.75)

*Price $1.95 in Canada

Buy them at your local
bookstore or use coupon
on last page for ordering.

Bestselling SIGNET VISTA Books

(0451)

☐ **GOODBYE, PAPER DOLL by Anne Snyder.** Seventeen, beautiful and bright, Rosemary had everything. Then why was she starving herself to death? (124332—$2.25)

☐ **COUNTER PLAY by Anne Snyder.** What does a guy do when he's straight and finds out his best friend isn't? Brad was faced with two choices—standing by his friend and losing a West Point appointment, or giving in to the disapproving pressure from his family, girlfriend, teammates and the whole town... (118987—$2.25)*

☐ **FIRST STEP by Anne Snyder.** Her mother's drinking problem was ruining Cindy's life—or was she ruining things for herself...? A novel about taking that all-important first step. (117573—$1.75)*

☐ **MY NAME IS DAVY—I'M AN ALCOHOLIC by Anne Snyder.** He didn't have a friend in the world—until he discovered booze and Maxi. And suddenly the two of them were in trouble they couldn't handle, the most desperate trouble of their lives.... (123360—$1.95)

*Prices slightly higher in Canada

Buy them at your local

bookstore or use coupon

on next page for ordering.

Bestsellers from SIGNET VISTA

(0451)

☐ YOU WANT TO BE WHAT? by Anne Snyder and Louis Pelletier.
(132203—$2.25)*

☐ THE BEST THAT MONEY CAN BUY by Anne Snyder and Louis Pelletier.
(125258—$2.25)*

☐ NOBODY'S BROTHER by Anne Synder and Louis Pelletier.
(117565—$2.25)

☐ TWO POINT ZERO by Anne Snyder and Louis Pelletier.
(114760—$1.75)*

☐ GOODBYE, PAPER DOLL by Anne Snyder.   (124332—$2.25)

☐ COUNTER PLAY by Anne Snyder.   (118987—$2.25)*

☐ FIRST STEP by Anne Snyder.   (117573—$1.75)*

☐ MY NAME IS DAVY—I'M AN ALCOHOLIC by Anne Snyder.
(123360—$1.95)*

☐ TWO BLOCKS DOWN by Jina Delton.   (114779—$1.50)*

☐ THE CLIFFS OF CAIRO by Elsa Marston.   (115309—$1.75)*

☐ OVER THE HILL AT FOURTEEN by Jamie Callan.   (130901—$1.95)*

☐ PLEASE DON'T KISS ME NOW by Merrill Joan Gerber. (115759—$1.95)*

☐ ANDREA by Jo Stewart.   (116542—$1.75)*

☐ ALICE WITH GOLDEN HAIR by Eleanor Hull.   (117956—$1.95)*

☐ A SHADOW LIKE A LEOPARD by Myron Levoy.   (117964—$2.25)*

*Prices slightly higher in Canada